13th Hour
Tales from Light to Midnight

By
Tammie Painter

Copyright © 2012
Tammie Painter & Black Rabbit Publishing
All rights reserved.
ISBN-13: 978-1479176175
ISBN-10: 1479176176

Table of Contents

Author's Introduction
Page 7

Part One - LIGHT

Hermes
Page 11

Bahati's Birthday
Page 23

Addiction
Page 30

Part Two - LOVE (or Not) IN THE AFTERNOON

Illusions
Page 39

Century Acres
Page 52

The Heron
Page 65

Feeding Suspicions
Page 73

Desmond, Casey and the Stonemason
Page 84

Part Three – EVENING

The Weaver
Page 95

Apple
Page 107

The Toad
Page 114

Family Secrets
Page 139

Part Four – MIDNIGHT

Island Ways
Page 148

Purge
Page 157

The Text
Page 164

Transcription of Taxi 6473
Page 171

L'Uomo Cotto
Page 186

Special Thanks to...
Page 196

About the Author
Page 197

Author's Introduction

Short stories provide many writers a chance to get an idea out of their head that may not work well as a full-fledged novel. In many cases, the stories in this book were inspired by random thoughts, weird dreams or – that most mundane of inspirations – an idea generated by a writing contest prompt. Certain stories such as "Feeding Suspicions" floated around in my head for months or years before getting put down on paper.

This book is broken up into four sections. In Light, you'll find three tales with quirky, yet happy endings. Love (or Not) in the Afternoon runs the gamut of unconventional love (and hate) stories – from what people will do for love to what people will do once they fall out of love. In Evening, things get a little darker and moodier. Midnight's five tales will leave you looking over your shoulder or taking a questioning look at your best friend and your favorite restaurant.

Because I love to find out what goes through authors' heads to inspire their work, each story begins with a short explanation of how the story came about.

Now, the sun is rising, it's growing light out, time for the 13th Hour.

Part One

LIGHT

Hermes

"Hermes" is a take on the myths surrounding the messenger god Hermes who later became the Roman god Mercury. The inspiration came from a writing contest that had something to do with boots flying across the room. Hermes wore winged sandals, but I thought just maybe he'd like a change in footwear. I pictured Hermes as being the go between an ever-horny Zeus, his favorite mortal Odysseus and Zeus's wife Hera. Anyone who's been an employee in a husband-and-wife run business will take this tale to heart.

W orking for the gods is never easy. Up here on Olympus, every task runs the risk of stepping on another god's toes. I should have known Zeus's chores would lead to trouble; I should have known none of his "problems" were accidental; and I should have known when Hera walked in that my day wasn't taking a turn for the better.

It all began with that idiot Perseus. How could he lose my winged sandals? Shows what happens when you trust a mortal with something valuable. Although Zeus is the one I should blame since it was he who insisted I "lend the lad something useful against the Gorgon" while fixing his gaze on my sandals. "They won't fit," I grunted, but he insisted. Now my wings rest at the bottom of the sea and Zeus's only response was to shrug and tell me "not to get upset over an old pair of footwear."

I commissioned Olympus's cobbler to construct a new pair of winged footwear. Boots this time. Sandals are ideal on Grecian land where the sun warms your skin, but up on Olympus or flying around, the biting cold sends my toes screaming. While cursing Perseus and Zeus for the loss of an heirloom, I looked forward to a warm pair of winged leather boots. Unfortunately, the cobbler's other work preceded mine. Aphrodite needed "something special" and, being higher on the Pantheon, she won the shoemaker's time.

Zeus caught me on my errand. "Hermes, have you heard?"

I probably had. The grapevine is long and well maintained on Olympus. Most news – gossip, I should say – is known by all before the initial report can ever be verified. Trying to guess which of the rumor mills Zeus was grinding would be impossible. "Heard what?"

"Of my poor Odysseus."

Oh, yes, this one. This was old news indeed. As Zeus's newest favorite mortal, all tongues are wagging about Odysseus lately. Word is that on his way home to Ithaca from a lengthy war (some skirmish over a girl, will these mortals never learn?) the man lost control of his ship and found himself stranded on the island of Ogygia – tiny, remote, not a bad place if one doesn't expect many amenities.

"Poseidon says he took no part in the matter, but I'm certain someone is playing a cruel joke on the man,"

Zeus went on shaking his head in disbelief with every word. We do love our jests with the mortals, but teasing any favorite of Zeus has become a competitive sport. It's hard to believe he's never caught on. "Now, my poor Odysseus is stuck on Ogygia with Calypso and she won't let him go."

As I said, I'd heard of Odysseus's "entrapment" before. It can't be all that bad and, in my opinion, he should stay. After all, it's been seven years; Odysseus isn't complaining about his fate and his wife certainly isn't sending out the search parties. Plus, being "stranded" with a nymph? How lucky could a prisoner get? I pulled my best attempt at a sympathetic face as Zeus spoke of how he thought it best for Ithaca if Odysseus could return.

"Go help the man, Hermes," he looked to my bare feet, "you've nothing better to do." I sighed to myself, not wanting to get involved in this. Unfortunately, he was right. I needed my "old pair of footwear" to do my job–seeing messages to their destinations and guiding the directionally-challenged deceased to the Underworld since, as much as mortals love their mates, having a dead spouse roaming about presents difficulties when bringing anyone new home. My winged helmet could get me from place to place, but I needed both helmet and sandals for my "god-ness" to be effective.

I searched for an argument against going, but you can't say "no" when you work for Zeus.

~ ~ ~

After years together, descriptions of Odysseus's flatulence, halitosis or impotence wouldn't sway Calypso; so I needed to bet on his lack of honesty. I stood by their bed and cleared my throat, but with their moaning and grunting it took me barking like a seal to distract them.

"What are *you* doing here?" Calypso hissed.

"Odysseus has to go." I told her.

"I'm not going anywhere," Odysseus announced while fondling Calypso.

"Zeus wants you home with Penelope." Odysseus's face whitened as Calypso slapped his hand away.

"Who's Penelope?" she screamed. The ocean churned in response to her anger.

"His wife," I said since Odysseus was too busy squirming to speak.

"You're married?" A wave bashing the shore emphasized her screech.

"Um, well a little. She could be dead for all I know."

"Penelope isn't dead," I sighed, "and hoards of men have been trying to have a go at her for years."

His eyes raged. Ignite the fire of jealousy and suddenly a man's wife is much more fascinating than any nymph. "Not my Pen—" I think he wanted to say more, but Calypso's smack across his face pushed the words back in.

"Get out of my sight," she said as she jutted her arm to indicate the door through which to leave.

We scurried away, more willing to face the tempest than its conjurer.

Poseidon agreed to help Odysseus to his boat, but refused to aid the mortal further. He advised me to do the same and to wash my hands of the troublesome human. I promised to try.

~ ~ ~

The instant I stepped in my door, Zeus hounded me.

"Hermes, please," he whined.

"Zeus, I've only just returned." I plopped into my favorite chair.

"No, up, up." He yanked me from my seat. "It's Io."

Io: Zeus's latest mortal consort - known as Flavor of the Month by the rest of us.

"What's wrong with Io? She's gorgeous and you've only had her three times. You can't be bored yet."

"No, I love her." Zeus loved all women, excepting his wife. His scattering of bastard half-breeds embarrassed the Greek Pantheon and each time a new one appeared we dreaded the additional work as Zeus insisted we watch over the child and bribe the Fates to its favor. "But Hera's angry."

"Who could blame her?" Hera was no wilting flower when it came to her husband's indiscretions.

"But she sent Argus to kidnap Io."

I struggled to contain my irritation. Here's my boss, the all-powerful head of the gods, and he can't muster the wit to snag his floozy away from a giant? Granted, it's a hundred-eyed giant under Hera's control, but he's *Zeus* for gods' sake.

"Let me guess, you want my help."

"Could you?" he asked brightly as if the question hadn't been on the edge of his lips.

"Fine, but once my boots are in, I'm going to be too busy for your nonsense."

"Understood."

Flute in hand, my tired helmet flew me to the beast. With Argus's hundred eyes fixated on Io, I played undetected and my lullaby sent him to sleep. Long story short, I cut off his head and carried Io home. She shrieked the entire way – apparently she'd grown to like the undivided attention from Argus and had issues with spurting blood. I dropped her at Zeus's door, not caring if it was he or Hera who answered.

Despite my exhaustion, I went to check on my boots hoping for their completion so I could escape any more of Zeus's chores.

"Sorry." The frazzled cobbler's hands buzzed as a string of gold threaded into a leather sole. "Aphrodite doubled her order. I won't finish your boots for days."

I groaned, but what could I do? I fluttered home to nap.

Zeus was already there.

"Haven't I done enough for one day?" Our days are quite long and mortal weeks might have passed since Zeus's first task. To say it had been a long day was no exaggeration.

"Odysseus is in trouble."

My bad mood over Aphrodite, Zeus's ineptitude and bone weariness took over.

"What, is *poor Odysseus* having to have sex with another gorgeous nymph?"

"Well—" he trailed off staring at his feet.

"Spill it."

"Circe."

"Oh no."

"Yep."

Circe, yet another nymph, lured men to her. She quickly got bored, but was too possessively jealous to send them off. As she couldn't have pestering suitors roaming around, she turned her jilted lovers into mice, elephants and an assortment of other beasts that scurried around her island as she tempted more men into her menagerie.

"What's she chosen for him?"

"Them. She wants to keep the crew he's obtained together."

"As?"

"Pigs."

Despite my exhaustion, I convulsed in laughter. Zeus started to plead, but I stopped him. "I'll go," I choked on the words as giggles spilled out, "but only to see the results if I'm too late."

My helmet beat its tired wings to Circe's sty, then kept me hovering me above the reeking muck seeping from the confines of the pen that had softened the surrounding ground into paste. Circe already managed to give the men corkscrew tails provoking my laughter once again. This task was well worth missing out on my much needed nap.

"You again?" Odysseus sneered.

"In the flesh. You'd think you'd just learn to set sail for home."

"The wind and waves brought me here."

"Sure, that and your loins. After this you're on your own." I tossed him a packet of herbs. "Eat these. They'll halt her spell." Circe, after pushing away an amorous lion, strode toward us grinning. "And by her smug expression, you better eat fast." They gobbled the herbs and the tails disappeared with a *pop*.

"Why are you here?" she grumbled.

"Nice to see you too, Circe. I found myself craving a ham."

She smiled thinking I was condoning her scheme. "Want to watch?"

"Sure."

She muttered a few odd phrases and nothing happened. After two more failed tries, the fabled temper I counted on sprang forth. She screamed, tore at her hair and stomped the ground. Her outrage plunged her waist deep into the muck. Odysseus and his men laughed cruelly as she continued to try the pig spell to no effect. I urged Odysseus to set sail straight to Ithaca.

"Perhaps," he shrugged.

I was done with him regardless of any further requests from Zeus.

Feeling guilty over the men's treatment of her, I helped Circe out of her mud stew and together we concocted a brilliant story to protect her reputation. The story told of Odysseus being too pig-like already for her magic to change him further; and, because of his insatiable fetish for devouring feces, she kept him around for several years to clean up the other animals' messes. With Odysseus's roaming ways I knew he wouldn't reach Ithaca for some time, thereby lending the tale an air of truth and Odysseus an interesting nickname for years to come.

~ ~ ~

Home again, I prayed there were no more troubled mortals in Zeus's sights and laid down to rest. The second I began to snore, Hera blasted my door away.

"You've helped *him*."

"Who?" I didn't know if she meant Zeus or Odysseus.

"The mortal. He doesn't want to return to Penelope. He deserves everything I'll do to him. Then, unlike other husbands, he'll appreciate being home and stay put."

Hera, constantly being put aside by Zeus, was always on the rampage against any of his mortal favorites, even the men. Being a chosen one of the gods isn't all it's cracked up to be because someone or some god will inevitably be jealous over the choice. Hera had been testing Odysseus to prove the mortal's unworthiness and because she resented Zeus's affection for the wandering husband. "And you helped the jerk." She stomped a golden-sandaled foot.

Again I was unsure to whom she referred.

"I work for Zeus and he commanded me. What could I do?"

"Spineless Hermes."

"No, wingless. Until I get my boots, which could be never if Aphrodite puts in another order, I'm left to your husband's whims."

"Not anymore." She threw one boot across the room and its heel wings fluttered for its maiden flight. It landed in my hand as the other flew to my side.

I put them on and they fit like they'd been formed to my feet. A glow washed over me knowing I was whole again - and that I wasn't at Zeus's bidding anymore. "A thousand thanks, Hera."

"There's a price." Her calculating voice erased my exhilaration. Of course, there was a price. Nothing was ever easy with the gods. "You've been thwarting my efforts all day. Twice with Odysseus and then with that slut Io. I was so pleased with myself for re-trapping Odysseus and getting Circe to turn him into what he really is – a rutting pig – and then my poor Argus. He was my favorite giant."

"Sorry, I didn't know. I wouldn't have—" I verbally and physically backed away. Of all the gods, I didn't want Hera angry with me.

"You have your boots back, so off to work with you."

I didn't trust her smirk.

"What's going on?"

"Orpheus."

"Please tell me he didn't."

Orpheus and Eurydice: a happier couple didn't exist. The gods should have looked to them for an example of marriage. They were truly a pair who would have lasted the ages. They were life for each other, the air the other breathed, the food the other ate. But one day, following Orpheus along a path, a snake bit Eurydice and she died. Orpheus's emotional life left him and I feared he'd taken his physical one as well.

"He's fine," she sighed. My relief at the news was only negated by my wariness of Hera's gift. "He bargained with one of us for one last day with Eurydice. She came out of the Underworld while you were off duty and they've had the most beautiful day together making love and gazing into each others' eyes," she oozed mocking sweetness.

"And now?"

"She has to go back. It's *your* job," she nodded to the boots, "to guide her."

"Can't she stay? He can't lose her again. Her death was a mistake."

"I do not make mistakes." The walls shook with her rage.

"*You* did it. *You* sent the snake. You couldn't stand to see a couple so happy, not with your miserable marriage full of revenge, contempt and jealousy."

She pointed at my broken door and said with poise, "You have a job to do Hermes."

"Yes, ma'am."

At the Gate to the Underworld, the couple embraced each other and cooed soft words in the other's ear. Separating them would rip their hearts apart. And mine. Hera's revenge for my day of undoing her work would be to burden me with the sadness of separating these two for the length of my existence. I watched them for a moment longer before telling the lovers it was time.

Glad to trail after his love even into death, Orpheus followed as I guided Eurydice.

I couldn't do it.

Let Hera torment the wayward Odysseus. Let Zeus ignore her. And let them all rot in Circe's sty. This day's work for the gods taught me a love like that of Orpheus and Eurydice needed to be saved.

At the threshold of the Gate, I clutched them to me and, shirking my duty for the first time in a millennium, flew across the Adriatic to the land gaining its own reputation for power. There, they could embrace the Roman gods and escape these petty Greek ones. The couple's joyful tears were thanks enough as I settled them into a prosperous village along the coast. I then turned my back on Greece forever to find a position in the Roman Pantheon.

Bahati's Birthday

This story came out of nowhere except my fascination for elephants and hatred of people who do bad things to them.

Struggling to her feet, the newborn elephant wobbled for a moment before staggering and falling once again. She shook her head, ears flapping into her eyes, then placed her two front feet squarely on the ground. The hour-old elephant pushed and rocked, readied her rear legs and hoisted herself into a swaying stand. Cautiously raising one foot, she took a step and stayed upright. Encouraged by this feat, she made three more steps to reach her mother. Desperate to suckle, the baby, like a pebble next to a boulder, sniffed its prostrate mother and backed away without realizing she hadn't mastered walking backwards. The calf collapsed, hungry and uncertain why her mother was so unwelcoming. She struggled to her feet again, then twitched her ears toward an approaching rumble.

John skidded the truck to a stop sending up a cloud of dirt. "We're just in time," he said as he jumped out.

The newborn elephant stood her ground, but stayed instinctively close to her mother.

The passenger door creaked open. "No, we're too late."

"Not if they haven't returned yet. Poachers would slobber over their rifles to get their hands on this cutie. She'd fetch tens of thousands in the exotic pet trade."

"Still," Ella, the preserve's newest volunteer, stooped down to pat the dead elephant, "the mother's dead."

"I should have known to keep an eye on her this close to her birthing time. Tutu was always like that - wandering off on her own, usually to visit her son Sam. It seems they never strayed too far from each other. With the boom in poaching incidents, we've got the herd under surveillance, but nothing indicated Tutu had roamed off. Her transmitter must have given out."

The baby raised her trunk to sniff Ella's face, blowing breath cooler than the African heat onto Ella's cheeks. The calf briefly drooped her trunk over Ella's shoulder then began to sniff her body.

"We better get her some food before she starts trying to nurse," Ella said.

"And before the poachers come back. They can't be far. Must have shot Tutu then gone trolling for any other easy pickings. Bastards. She needs to feed first though. There's formula and a bottle in the truck. We can figure out where the herd is on the monitor. After she eats we can transport her back to them."

It didn't take much to convince the miniature elephant to follow. Despite feeling drawn to the body, the hungry animal sensed she would get nothing from her fallen, strangely scented mother. With a few pushes on her rump, she let the man guide her back to the truck. The vehicle was an odd smelling creature, but the calf had already scented similar traces of metal, oil and rubber on the woman.

The creak of the truck's back end opening gave the newborn a start and she trotted over to Ella on legs that each seemed to have its own agenda. John grinned, "Looks like you have a new friend."

"I can see how someone would want one at this age, but in a year?" Ella asked as she patted the elephant's head.

John filled the oversized bottle with the condensed milk formula developed by the preserve for orphaned elephants. Too many calves lost their mothers to poachers' guns and traps not to have a back up plan if the preserve workers could get to the babies in time. He snapped on the nipple - a cross between a latex glove and swimming cap. After squirting out a bit of formula that disappeared into the parched earth, John presented the bottle to the newborn. She explored the bottle for a few seconds with her trunk before clamping onto the nipple with her mouth. Trickles of formula dribbled along her stone-colored cheek as she gulped down the rich drink.

Ella was right; it was always tempting to keep the calves. The preserve had plenty of land for the elephants to grow up with space to roam and other elephants to bond with. The problem was too many "collectors," as they liked to call themselves, purchased baby elephants, gave them no exposure to their own kind and, after a year or two of rapid growth, found they hadn't planned for the amount of room or food an elephant required. Lucky elephants ended up being handed over to a preserve; some were sold to circuses. But too many ended up dead from either malnutrition or depression - or a gunshot to rid the "collector" of the burden. John hoped they could find the herd to let this newborn live a normal elephant life. But first she needed another bottle.

As Ella prepared the second serving, a branch snapped. She froze. John's hand went to the nearest weapon – a tranquilizer gun at his hip. He tucked behind the open passenger side door and scanned the area. Ella moved with the baby to the other side of the vehicle and crouched down.

"What was that?" she whispered.

John's eyes darted over the surrounding brush, but saw nothing. All was silent except for the usual midday bird calls. He shrugged, "Must have just been a branch falling. Give her that second bottle and let's get out of here."

"I've got a serious case of the creeps," Ella said as the elephant huddled closer.

John felt it too. Something deep in his spine screamed with tension urging him to get moving. He looked to Ella, the calf was halfway through the second bottle. He was about to go over to them when the click of a rifle being cocked stopped him in his tracks.

"That's ours," said a man who'd covered the lower half of his face with a bandana as if in the Old West. "Hand it over and we'll let you go."

Two black men, wearing bandanas and bearing pistols, approached to back up the white man.

John's stomach rumbled and the sensation brought back the spine-deep tension. He'd experienced this feeling once before and now recognized the instinctive warning he'd ignored. The baby elephant, even with no knowledge of the world, also had instinct enough to recognize something was wrong and pressed herself against the truck's wheel well. Trying not to move too quickly, John eased closer to the vehicle.

"Hey," the white man yelled, "hold it there or—"

Before he could finish the threat, a bull elephant stampeded out of the brush. He'd quit sending the stomach rumbling subsonic warnings, and now bellowed his approach. Pistol and rifle shots went off as the male galloped toward the three poachers who scurried into a run. With the white man in second place between the two black men, the poachers ran without looking back.

The trailing black man tripped as he tried to turn to shoot at the elephant. As he charged after the other two poachers, the bull's feet crunched the bones in the fallen man's back. Without bothering to aim, the leading black man fired his pistol behind him three times. Two shots went wild, but one pierced the white man's skull, sending him to the ground in a heap.

Taking a few lunging strides, the bull crashed into the pistol-wielding man. The poacher clawed at the ground to scramble away. The elephant turned, charged again and trampled the man's head under a dinner plate-sized foot.

Snorting and huffing with exertion, the bull lumbered over to the fallen female. For several minutes, he bowed his head low sniffing and petting her body with his trunk.

John and Ella stayed as still as possible. The baby made no sound or movement around the big, strange male. Finally, the bull finished his ritual, gave the vehicle a sideways look while sniffing the air before he traipsed back into the brush.

John jumped when the baby elephant sniffed at his hand looking for another bottle. Ella went to the back looking as white as the few thin clouds in the sky. She said nothing as she prepared a bottle with trembling hands. The baby gulped it down, unbothered by anything but a renewed hunger now that the male had left.

"Was that the father?" Ella asked as she stared at the baby's long-lashed eyes.

"No, that was Sam, Tutu's son. Seeing and smelling his mother's body must have set him off. She almost done with that?"

A sucking gurgle from the bottle answered his question.

"Let's get her measured and tagged and in the truck to find the herd so her aunties can take care of her."

"Will they accept her? They won't reject her, will they?"

"Two are nursing calves and will take turns caring for this little one. Elephants always seem to want something to nurture," John grinned for the first time since the branch snapped. "They're worse than Irish grannies. I swear, if they could, they'd probably make tea and biscuits for her."

Ella took notes as John measured the elephant's ear size, foot diameter, height and length. Distracted by another bottle, the calf merely swatted her tail when John injected a mini-transmitter under the skin between her shoulders. Ella pointed at the form, to the space next to the transmitter number.

"Name?" she asked.

John thought for a moment.

"Bahati." He spelled it out as she wrote.

"What's it mean?"

"Lucky."

Addiction

"Addiction" came about two ways. One, from a dream I had about sitting down and having a chat over beers with Anthony Bourdain – I seriously didn't want the dream to end, but yet can't remember a damn thing we were talking about. And two, from working for seven years as a chemist in a neuroscience research laboratory where we studied how addiction affects the brain.

I envy people with easy cravings that can be fed on almost any street corner.

Not so for me. I'm an addict chasing the dragon I thought could never be caught: dreams.

Just as some people are hooked after one drag on a coffin nail or ride on the Horse, I can't dream without being left with the hand-shaking jonesing for "just one more." Everyone's had them, those dreams where upon waking you will yourself to fall back to sleep hoping for the dream to continue. Well, I *need* the dream to continue.

The ones that leave me cursing the rising sun like a modern day Nosferatu are surreal, simple, and, yes, sometimes sexual. An espresso and chat with a long dead author or actor (albeit in a mish mash-only-exists-in-dreams ramshackle house where the owner misplaced her pet ducks), a tour through Rome with no one around except the ghost-hosts of dead gladiators and emperors, the kiss of a stranger I can't find again, or the espionage dream where I almost save the world (were it not for the real-world cat pawing at my head to be fed). I'm pulled from these by the daylight and yearn to return.

Like the alcoholic barely sobering up for the workday and counting the minutes until happy hour, my life has become a long series of waking hours.

I started learning how to bring on the best dreams, the blissful escapes from the real world. It didn't take long to notice a glass or two of wine before bed delivered my sleeping mind to a vivid world. It wasn't alcoholism. If it weren't for the dreams the noble rot induced, I could care less about my glass being filled. Still, my spouse became concerned when I began going through my box-o-wine (the cheaper the wine, the better the dreams) in a week.

I then discovered the subconscious wonder world of Nyquil. I remembered the bizarre nightly plays I'd have as a child when my mom would dose me up with the thick unearthly green liquid. Half a dose was enough and I could sneak my sip before hopping into bed where I urged my mind to quiet its waking thoughts and allow me back into my preferred realm. Empty bottles were easily disposed of in my company's recycling bins and a new bottle could be picked up from the drug store on the way home. Problem solved. Lovely dreams and no more nagging about needing to "see someone about my drinking."

With the knowledge of what alcohol could do, it didn't take a great leap of curiosity to wonder what visions stronger drugs could bring. The lab my sister manages studies addiction. She's the only one I've told about my cravings.

"You're an addict." Her eyes lit up with the diagnosis.

"What? You want to study me?"

"My sibling guinea pig," she cooed and it was tough to tell if she was mocking or serious.

"I just want some of your stuff."

Her research centers on coke and meth. Stimulants wouldn't help me, but over years of waiting for grants to come through, she has concocted some of the best LSD this side of the Willamette. And being around college students meant unlimited access to pot.

"What effects do you expect?" I'd become no better than one of her mice.

"I'll let you know," I replied.

I was disappointed.

The pot only made me sleep. No dreams, just a strange feeling in my mouth. Not an experience to feed an addiction. The LSD had so much potential but never delivered the coherent and focused dreams I wanted, only a series of swirls and percussions of reality. I suppose it's better that way. After all, if I couldn't even drink a few glasses of wine without being harassed, what would have happened if I was dropping acid each night before tucking in? I reported to my sister and picked up an economy size bottle of Nyquil on the way home.

I can't give it up - the dreams, not the Nyquil. If I could have the subconscious intensity without the green goo, I'd gladly give up that sickening antifreeze-like stuff. But I yearn to get back to that espresso, to my superhero/spy antics, to one more kiss, to explore another alleyway with the gladiators.

After a while, eight hours proved to not be enough.

I started napping in the lounge at work during lunch. Instructions from a website on power napping worked better than warm milk. A jigger of Nyquil, a few repetitive phrases, and I was out.

Then that hour wasn't enough. I'd wake up angry because the good part of whichever fantasy world I entered had just begun. I took it out on my secretary one day and she reported me. One reprimand was no big deal with my work record, but when my naps started at ten and ran until two my boss took notice. Yet another reprimand, but being a junkie I ignored the negative consequences of my addiction. I had to get back. Someone in the dream needed me there, wanted me there. Who else in the waking world could understand me so well?

There were no further reprimands. I was fired without severance.

My job status was easy to hide at first. I'd leave the house in the morning – Nyquil in tote – and head to the park or public library depending on the weather. Librarians and police woke me on occasion, but for the most part I could dream away for up to six wonderful hours.

My unemployment didn't go unnoticed for long. There's only so long you can hide a lack of income when you have a joint checking account and the mortgage is due.

For the lie, not for the job loss, I was dumped.

"I had such great dreams for us," was all my dear one said before closing the door. I didn't mind. I could dream about her anytime I wanted.

The following weeks brought me exceptional visions. I slept great having the bed to myself. I no longer woke up cold from the covers being yanked off or balancing on the mattress edge while someone sprawled across the bed. I could take my wine without guilt or nagging and celebrated the end of my Nyquil consumption.

I dreamt. I slept. I was happy.

But it couldn't last.

It's not that I had a problem with my sloth. I was content in my dream world, but the mortgage company expected payment I couldn't deliver.

I lost the house. My bed went with me to my sister's.

One night the television aired a program on coma patients. Researchers stated that, despite conventional wisdom, the patients were showing brain wave patterns similar to people in a dream state. I never knew I could be so interested in comas.

"How do people end up in comas?" I asked.

"Usually major trauma to the brain – injuries, infections, overdose. I think of it as the brain shutting down the body to protect itself."

I couldn't imagine darting in front of a car to achieve what I was thinking. There was too much risk for ending up dead. But a coma, a way to always dream. How wonderful.

"They can induce comas, right?"

"Sure, generally to reduce pressure in the brain."

"What if someone wanted to be induced?"

"Your life's not that bad. Besides, no one is going to 'treat' you now that you don't have insurance."

"You have access to hospital resources. You could do it as part of an experiment."

"You're crazy. Why would you do this?"

"You've spent years researching addiction."

"But most people's dreams don't bring about a dopamine surge capable of causing addiction." She spoke sternly, but as the words came out, she realized the potential. The glint in her eyes gave away the interest she was trying to hide.

"Exactly, so study me. Take me as a research subject. Knock me out, hook me up and analyze my brain. Hell, you can even shave my head and stick probes in like you do with your mice. Whatever. Just let me dream."

She was hooked. The novelty of the concept was too much to resist. She arranged for me to spend three nights in a sleep lab to obtain a baseline reading and then bribed a physician to induce and monitor me. My darling sister padded the grants to fund my care.

Now, everything has been prepared. Today is my last day in the conscious realm. I told her to keep me under until the project couldn't be funded any longer. It could be ten days. It could be ten years. I should want to walk in the park, go to the zoo, bungee jump, something. I don't. I just want to dream.

The lights are dimming. My coma begins any second now. I shut my eyes waiting to be satiated. My addiction finally satisfied.

As the light of my consciousness fades, I've never been happier.

Part Two

LOVE (or Not)

IN THE AFTERNOON

Illusions

"Illusions" started out simple enough, with a contest that required the first line be "My life is a sham." I wanted to write a quirky love story, but didn't want any cliché ideas. The economy was in the tank and I thought how could a person make money that would be a sham to their normal existence. Somehow, drag queen *was one of the first in the brainstorm list.*

"My life is a sham."

Staring into the bathroom mirror, I say this to myself every afternoon upon waking. With the late nights at the club I haven't seen morning for some time. I miss the calm of dawn – waking up to it, rather than going to sleep to it – and the ritual of coffee as birds make the only sound. Waking in the afternoon, the world is up and mowing, driving, chatting and drowning out the sounds of nature with every chance it gets.

My training, my experience, my past life was as a naturalist, or "Wildlife Biologist III" to use the government's job title. I loved nature so much I wanted to spend my life studying and telling others about it, but cuts to grants pushed me out of a career. I was downsized out of my real life.

I tried other jobs, but sitting at a desk all day typing meeting minutes and entering someone else's data made me miserable. I should have been entering my own data and writing journal articles. I'm great at taking things apart, putting them back together, not so much – possibly too much time spent dissecting things - so a typical manly job with tools and mechanical bits would never work. I can draw pretty well, but artists are about as employable as scientists these days. I even flipped burgers for a while. A PhD and I'm flipping all-beef (so they say) patties. I quit after the first paycheck and spent the next week scrubbing the smell of grease from my hair.

Retail? I spent my career trying to preserve nature and reduce our impact on it. How could I sell out to promote conspicuous consumption? Quite easily it seems when the mortgage loomed over me like an elephant's foot over a dung beetle. I thought perhaps the department store would hire me to sell electronics or garden tools. Instead, the store manager believed I'd do best in cosmetics. I didn't know blush from bronzer, but she insisted.

"You say you need money and the commission is best there. With all the formulas and ingredients it's kind of scientific." She arched her too-black eyebrows waiting for an agreeing nod from me, but she didn't need one. She had made her choice for my future and I needed the cash too badly to argue. "Besides, your face will attract the ladies. Those eyes and cheekbones will draw them in like flies to honey."

In a pretense of looking knowledgeable enough to tell women about toner and SPF, I donned my store-issued white lab jacket. It wouldn't be the last costume I'd put on to make money, but this one came with my name embroidered across the breast pocket.

It wasn't bad. I was moving around and getting to talk to and flirt with attractive women. One day though, the customers weren't coming. Stocks plummeted the day before and I think everyone was too financially nervous to go shopping. My co-worker, Sally, alphabetized the eye shadows and I dusted every corner of the displays. By eleven a.m. boredom overwhelmed us.

"Let's do your make-up," she said making a tick mark on a scrap of paper to denote the passing of another fifteen minutes.

"Um, Sally, I'm a guy. Just putting that out there in case you hadn't notice."

"Yeah, but you've got a great face. Every woman would kill to have your eyelashes and lips. C'mon, you can wash it right off."

I debated. I was bored, but was I bored enough to have my colors done in the middle of a public area? What if my ex-wife walked in? Wait, no one was walking in. What the hell, why not?

"Fine, but do it quick. And none of that god awful purple or anything Day-Glo."

"Don't worry, you'll be so beautiful I'll have to start hating you." She patted her chair indicating for me to sit and indulge her whim.

So I sat. Sally smoothed moisturizer and a light foundation over my face as I marveled over the turn my vocabulary had taken. The sweeping of the blusher and puff of powder tickled, but I obeyed Sally's orders not to sneeze. I worked at stretching my face just right for her to apply the eye makeup and then looking up far enough to get the mascara on without smudging. Embarrassing as it potentially could be, it felt good to have attention paid to me and I realized now why the women Sally finished with walked away bearing a glow as if they were the queens of the earth.

Sally stood back and admired her handiwork.

"You're pretty," she gushed. "Oh, here." She grabbed a women's hat – a sequined number with a feather - from the rack across the counter and fixed it onto me.

I scowled at her. "This was not part of the deal."

"Oh, but you're divine."

"Okay, enough." I started to pull the hat off.

"Wait," a husky voice commanded from behind. Sally's eyes widened as her toothy smile transformed to a slack O.

I turned and, worrying one of the managers had caught us, moved to finish removing the hat.

"No, leave it," the jowly man commanded. I knew who he was, everyone in Portland knew him. This unattractive mound of a fellow owned, managed, and performed at Illusions, Portland's first and still most popular venue for cross-dressing acts. This man, Carl Dylan – a.k.a. Desiree Carlotta - who right now sported a heavy five o'clock shadow, covered his face in a few layers of makeup (I wondered in a flash if Sally ever did his colors), seated one of his many elaborately coiffed wigs on his head, donned as many sequins as possible and put on a top rate variety show.

From what I heard anyway.

I'd never been to Illusions. I didn't have anything against it, to each his own, but I never understood the attraction of watching men dress up as women. Except for Monty Python and Kids in the Hall, of course.

A meaty hand took my chin and tilted my head gently one way and then the next making judgmentally approving sounds. He let me go and pulled out a business card as he eyed the name embroidered on my left breast pocket.

"Ray, you've got a great face. Got any other talents?"

Sally nudged me. I'd told her too much about myself not to have her spill the beans if I didn't confess. My mom, not liking the wild nature boy her son was becoming, sought to tame him by teaching me something refined.

"I play piano."

"Well?"

"Well what? You asked."

"No, do you play well?"

"Oh, sorry, yeah, I guess so."

"Auditions are Tuesday nights. Come fully dressed." I cringed knowing he meant in full drag. "If you make it you get $200 a night for a four-hour set. You do the math, probably a little more than you make here.

If people like you, sometimes you'll get tips as well. See you Tuesday."

And he turned to leave. Just like that. As if I had no questions. As if performing in drag was the next step I'd been hoping to take on my career ladder.

Sally spun me around to face her. The invasion of my personal space over the past several minutes was getting out of hand.

"You are totally doing this," she urged.

"No, I am totally not." I finally pulled off the hat, scooted away from her and grabbed a bottle of makeup remover.

"Ray, that's fifty bucks an hour, just to play the piano."

"Not *just* play the piano. Play a piano in a dress."

"And heels. You'll have to shave your legs too. It's way easier than your face I've heard." Sally was already sending me to the she-wolves.

"No."

"Fifty an hour, plus tips. Ray, you're making minimum wage here plus a little commission *selling* makeup. You could triple that by *wearing* the makeup. I could get you the makeup for free and it would be easy to 'borrow' dresses from Formal Wear."

"And the size ten stilettos too, I suppose?"

"Oh you don't want to go the stiletto route at first," she said as if I was seriously contemplating my wardrobe.

I gave her an *are-you-being-serious* look.

"Besides," she continued, "it'd be hard to play piano in stilettos. The heels would get scuffed from working the pedals. A wedge would be better."

Of course Sally goaded me into auditioning. For this occasion we didn't pilfer-then-return to the store – although that would become the *modus operandi* for my performances. For the audition Sally handed me a slinky number I would have killed to see her in. She told me she got it for a trip to Vegas with a boyfriend that never panned out – the trip nor the boyfriend. She did my makeup, padded my bra, and slipped a pink bobbed wig on my head.

"From Vegas?" I asked about the wig.

"No, just for fun." I found myself having an unexpected crush on Sally as she scanned me critically. "You're going to have to take care of that," she nodded toward my crotch. "I only do makeup."

"Take care?"

"Tuck."

I looked in the mirror at the slight bulge and blushed. A few minutes in the bathroom and I met Sally's approval.

Carl was at the audition. He sat in the back in men's clothes smoking a cigarette, looking more gangster than cross dresser. The contrast of wearing black sequins and hot pink hair and playing Beethoven's Fur Elise sent my audience – ten men in drag – raving. They all lamented it was "ironically beautiful" although I wondered if they appreciated the music when one said he/she "just *loved* Mozart."

I took their applause and admiration over my "stunning" attire with all the grace I could. I didn't know how to act. Here were ten men I knew to be men but gushing over me like a pack of over-enthusiastic aunties. What could I do? When in Rome, as they say. I gushed in equal amount over their dresses while trying not to think about the amount of tucking they'd done. Carl whooshed them away after a few minutes and told me to sit down at one of the tables

"You want this job?" he asked.

"It's not my dream job, but the money is good." The oddity of wearing a dress and speaking with my tenor voice threw me off for a second. "And mom would be proud. I'm finally using those piano lessons," I quipped.

"You're straight, right?"

Damned if a flashing image of Sally didn't parade across my brain.

"Yeah, is that a problem?"

"I'm gonna level with you," he took a long drag and then exhaled up and away from my face. "I'm straight. Most people don't know that."

Carl/Desiree is coming out to me? Could my life get any stranger? Everyone in Portland, whether they approved, disapproved or didn't give a rat's ass assumed Carl was gay.

"Well, okay," I said, my voice indicating the *do-you-have-a-point* thought tramping through my head.

"These ladies," his head gestured toward the back stage to where my audience went, "are gay, or well, they," he stumbled over his words. "I don't know - they're confused. When I started this club it was just a bunch of us being silly, but these days— Well, I don't know what these boys are. They're gay is all the best I can describe it. Some date each other." He seemed repulsed at the idea. Carl/Desiree was a homophobe? The local media would have a field day. "I thought maybe some, you know, just 'identified' as women. But most of these boys are just out and out gay."

"Okay." Again, what was his point?

"I'm telling you now you need to keep your sexual orientation to yourself. Sort of the don't ask don't tell policy, but if they ask you need to lie."

I laughed. He couldn't be serious. Talk about reverse discrimination.

"No," he stubbed out his cigarette, "I'm serious. They accept that I'm not one of them. Actually I play it off saying I'm too old for them or that I don't swim in the company pool, but some of them suspect. Many of them've received a bad hand from straight men - disapproving fathers, abusive uncles, that sort of thing. If they know you're straight they will make your life miserable. I've seen it; it ain't pretty. If you think women can be catty you've never seen a room of ticked off gay cross dressers. You've seen Cujo?"

"Read the book."

"Well, believe me, Stephen King's got nothing on how these ladies can be."

"You're serious?"

"They'll castrate you, honey. No exaggeration. Play the part, earn your money and keep quiet."

I can't say I wasn't nervous my first night. A Friday night with a sold out show and the nerves weren't coming from the idea of playing the piano in drag, but instead festered from the notion of being trapped in a twenty-by-twenty dressing room with a pack of narrow-minded men. It would be the same feeling I'd have if I walked into a redneck bar wearing a Democratic Convention tee shirt.

"Hey newbie, which one of us you like the best?" asked a Hispanic girl/boy in a red feathered dress.

Play the part or lose your parts, rang through my head. I forced myself to calm down to keep from sweating off Sally's hard work.

"Um," I scanned the room. Even if I were gay none of these guys would appeal to me. Too skinny trying to look 'feminine'. "Wow, I can't decide. It's like I'm in a candy shop."

That lame line garnered a chorus of giggles.

"But which of us are you going to do first, Raylene?" The whole room turned its sequins and eyelashes toward me.

Oh hell. I needed to play this as politic as I could.

"Sorry, but I'm spoken for. My partner and I have been together for ages."

A sigh emanated from the room.

"Are y'all gettin' married?" twanged one of the girls.

"Oh, you know the laws," I affected a gay lisp from out of nowhere. "We get married, then we're not married. I think we've been hitched about five times now."

"Ooh, is he gonna be here tonight?"

Sally was going to be here. My heart pounded at the thought. How could I work with someone for three months and the thing that sends me gushing over her like a teenager is wearing her dress and makeup?

"Um, no, he knows I get nervous in front of him"

"Oh I know *exactly* how that goes. I could do a lap dance for the President, but if my mom walked in on one of my shows I'd freeze."

I was off the hook for a while. I played well and thanked Sally for "borrowing" the size ten wedges from the store with every pedal push. The whole thing was surprisingly fun until I got back in the dressing room and saw what the lights and sweat had turned me into - an old cocktail waitress at a shabby Vegas casino. My music was beautiful and catchy and fun, but every night I performed I knew I was living a lie. The "girls" would tear me apart if they discovered what I was and my situation left me afraid to ask Sally out.

The money, however, kept me in the game. I was making $4,000 a month, not counting tips. Thanks to the eclectic tastes of the piano teacher my mom hired, I knew a bit of everything and my ability to play any request skyrocketed my salary and popularity. Unless a ravenous gang of cross dressers killed me for duping them for four months, I was doing all right.

Still, I grew to love Sally more and more. I desperately looked forward to every second she did my make up, and refused her offers to teach me how to apply my own eye shadow to look best under the harsh limelight by insisting her hand was steadier. Every swish of the blusher and puff of air to clear off excess powder sent shudders down my spine. I wanted to kiss her as she applied the final coat of mascara, but feared she'd scold me for mussing my lipstick.

I woke up every afternoon telling myself my life was a sham.

I was hopeless and sick of the ruse. But the money was too good to turn back.

"Sally," I started hesitantly one evening as she applied concealer over a zit brought on by stress, "can I ask you something?"

"Sure, anything. I've seen you tuck, there's no secrets between us."

I hated the *we're-old-girlfriends* tone in her voice. Was I ridiculous to think she might like me?

"Well, I was wondering if you want to go out sometime." My cheeks burned.

She looked at me like I was a winged goat that sprouted out of the tomato plant she tended on her balcony. Not the look I was hoping for.

"Sorry, I shouldn't have asked. Just friends, I get it."

"No," she said. "Oh Ray, I thought maybe you, well, maybe," she flourished her hand over me.

"What, you think I'm gay?"

"Well, you're divorced, no girlfriend, and you took to this job so easily."

"At *your* goading. And if you recall it was your boredom that got me the audition. I'm divorced because my wife ran off with an investment banker after only a year of trying to live on a scientist's wages. No, Sally, I am one hundred percent straight and I think about you every day and dream about you every night."

"All this time I just wrote you off as my gay friend. I mean, I can't say I didn't really wish you weren't, but you're not?"

"No, there's just one complication," I brushed my hand over her hair.

~ ~ ~

I stared out to the audience and felt a glow as I saw the person I loved.

"I thought your guy didn't come around to the shows," said Marcus/Mariana.

"We're trying something new."

"Gotcha," he/she winked. "Well, keep him away from backstage, all the girls want a piece of that. Good job on snagging that one."

"Um, thanks."

The lights dimmed and the show was on.

I couldn't keep my eyes off Sally. I loved her. I even imagined proposing during a show - but for now I just stared at her. She looked so beautifully cute with her hair cropped short, no makeup and dressed in my jeans and blazer. She winked at me and I played on.

Century Acres

This is another story that started out as a contest, but took on a life of its own. I forget what the original first line was supposed to be, but it was something about Paul and Miriam Kaufman. This sounded like such a pair of old folks' names that I thought it would be interesting if they were two old people living in a retirement home who have the same last name, but don't know each other. I began to picture Miriam having a huge crush on Paul like a teenage girl. Over revisions, the names changed and the story grew. It's a light, loving take on a serious disease.

"We need to talk."

"It's a cockamamie idea and I'm not discussing it."

"It'll be better for you, Dad. You'll be around people who know how to care for you and you'll have friends your own age to talk to."

"Just what I want, extra time with a bunch of grumpy old farts." Twenty years ago Ella insisted her father move from the East Coast town he'd lived in for five decades telling him she could care for him in Portland. Now she was sending him away. Paul knew that husband of hers was behind it; his Ella would never abandon him like this. "Why would I wanna be around people who're gonna die in their sleep the day after I meet them?"

"Dad, this isn't easy. If you get care now—" she trailed off.

"Care for what?" Paul scoffed. "Forgetting a few things? Just a brain fart."

"You forgot Jacob's name."

"Jacob who?"

"My husband, Jacob." Ella's panic vanished at the sight of her father's teasing grin. "It's not funny, Dad. This is serious. These people can help."

Paul doubted it. He knew Alzheimer's. He'd feared it since he'd first heard the term. He knew being locked away with a bunch of fuddy-duddies and under-trained attendants wouldn't help. He ought to travel, stimulate his mind as they say. Screw word problems and Sudoku, he wanted adventure. He could do it; he had the means. Even Ella didn't know about that. Whenever he brought up going somewhere on his own Ella would refuse and argue: "What if you can't remember where you are or how to get back?"

To which he always responded: "I'll find a friendly local girl to watch over me."

The last time they had the argument, rather than roll her eyes, Ella handed him the brochure for Century Acres. The glossy piece of propaganda made it look like a swank hotel where the company holiday party might be held, but Paul knew the brochure for the animal shelter gave the same impression. And look what happened to those inmates - either adopted and saved or sent to chase the great chew bone in the sky.

Paul fought it, but that Jacob must have swayed Ella to get rid of him.

And so, four months ago, Paul was left on the steps of Century Acres like a mutt being ditched at the pound. Ella came by three times a week that first month, then once a week, and now – to be honest, he didn't recall how long it had been and it sent shivers through him. Had she been here and he didn't remember, or had she simply stopped coming? Either option was terrible to consider.

~ ~ ~

There he is sulking, always sulking. Flipping the pages of his *National Geographic Traveler* and chewing on his lip as he always does, never settling on any one page. I know what he's going though. He hasn't had a visitor since the first of May. I used to wish I had a daughter, thinking they were more caring, more loyal, and would never abandon a parent. But here he is, left in this place just as I was by my ingrate son.

I was never any trouble to him. Just that one day I walked out of the condo with no pants – or underwear. Someone called the cops and, after they'd gotten a towel around my bum, I had a little trouble remembering the condo's number.

"It's that building there," I pointed, "The Henry. I'll figure out which apartment it is once I get back inside, if you don't mind."

They did mind and the doorman – I never did like him, not for his color mind you, but because he always flirted with the girls in the building as if a woman living in a million dollar condo would take up with a doorman regardless if he's black, pink, or green – gave the police my son's number.

And do you know what he said? The dear boy I fed and cleaned and educated wasn't concerned about my health or my mental state at all. When he came to get me at the station, he didn't ask if I was okay or why I was out with no bottoms (I swear I put them on, no wonder it felt so drafty). All he said was, "I hope none of my friends saw you." All snotty-like.

Well, I had to reply. "Why, worried they might want to ask a looker like me out on a date?"

And that started it.

"I think it's time you found a care facility."

"An old folks' home, you mean? You don't have to be politically correct around me, I've heard what you call the doorman."

"You need to be somewhere where people know how to deal with you."

"Because I walked out without my pants?"

"For the third time, Mother."

Had it been? He must be making that up. And he knows it irks me when he calls me *Mother* in that tone.

"Fine," I huffed, "I'll pack tonight."

The next day he took me to Century Acres and hasn't visited since. Although he does call now and then, but only on weekends so as to not "waste his minutes." Whatever that means.

I'd been here about a month when I saw Paul being dropped off like a scared and grumpy child at his first day of kindergarten. I thought he was the bee's knees the second I saw him haul – on his own, mind you - three suitcases from the curb and on up the stairs to his room.

I hoped I wouldn't forget him. And do you know what? I didn't.

Each day I'd seek him out and sit across from him as he read a travel magazine and chewed on his lip. And one day a funny thought crept into my head that I'd like to chew on his lip too. My giggle drew attention from the attending nurse.

"Mrs. Cohen, everything alright?" She eyed me warily as if I might go on a rampage because I wasn't being morose like the other recliner-dwelling dullards here.

"What? We're not allowed to have funny thoughts? I was under the impression that not thinking was the bad thing."

She shot me daggers with her eyes. "I'm only being concerned."

And I thought, You only want to up my meds and knock me out to make your job easier. But that kind of talk would get me nowhere so I just said, "Of course, dear."

When I looked back, Paul was staring at me with his devilish green eyes and I could tell from the still-dark fringe of lashes that his hair had been black before it turned its current steely gray.

~ ~ ~

Paul watched the exchange between the nurse and the woman. He'd noticed this petite woman try to speak to him a few times, but he didn't want any friends so each time he pretended to be enthralled with his reading. What was the point of meeting anyone in Century Acres? He pondered the irony of being locked away and forgotten by a daughter who complained about his forgetfulness. Why meet anyone else, especially in a place where the people were guaranteed to forget you in a year, a month, hell, even a day? Who could say how long any of their memories would hold out? He endured the nurses' encouragement and when the doctors asked for drug trial volunteers Paul signed up figuring life as a guinea pig would at least give him something to do.

Paul didn't want to admit it also gave him hope. Hoping seemed pointless in a place like Century Acres. With its supposedly soothing color scheme, stale scent of the elderly and falsely chipper staff, most things seemed pointless at Century Acres. So he withdrew into his travel magazines and books, dreaming of where he could be while the woman sat across from him on the verge of speaking, but halted by his interest in the pages.

But when the nurse addressed the woman as Mrs. Cohen and he saw the woman's underlying desire to smart mouth back (oh, he recognized the look and knew she was holding back a zinger), he had a strange moment of curiosity and a feeling he hadn't experienced in four months: Paul wanted to meet someone.

"My name's Cohen too," he said cringing at the sound of his own voice. It sounded so old, so gruff. And to think he'd been good at flirting with the ladies in his day.

~ ~ ~

My face burned. Paul was speaking to me. Oh, I hope he hadn't read my earlier thought about his lips. It's like ages ago when I'd go to the dance halls and chat up any plain fellow who looked my way, but if the handsomest man in the room asked me to dance I'd be too nervous to give anything other than mumbled one-word responses. That's probably why I ended up with such a homely husband. Now the most attractive man I've seen in years is speaking to me and I feel like I'm back at the dances. Only now I know I need to reply before he thinks I'm one of the Century Acres Crazies.

~ ~ ~

The woman stared at him. Paul wondered if this one already had her mind eaten away by the Big A. But after a long pause she spoke.

"I know. I thought it was funny when I first learned your last name was Cohen too. My late husband was Jewish, it drove my Catholic mother to her wit's end." She smiled and Paul thought his heart was troubling him before recalling the drop and thud in the chest at the realization a crush was in the making. He was too old to have a crush, wasn't he?

"My name's Vivian. And you're Paul."

"You seem to know a lot about me, Vivian."

"Not much more than your name," she paused. "And that, like me, you don't have many visitors."

He wanted to hold back. It was rude to gripe to a stranger, but she didn't seem unfamiliar to him and the words he'd been holding back for four months tumbled out. "Kids are rotten. You think they'd treat us better. I worked, sent her to school, made the down payment on her first house and what do I get in return? My freedom taken away. I wanted to go here," he stabbed at the magazine cover, "and instead I end up in this place. I'm sorry, Vivian. I sound like a bitter old fool."

"You've every right to be, Paul."

She smiled at him and his heart trotted through his chest again.

~ ~ ~

I loved saying his name and I loved how my name sounded coming off his lips. Each day we talked more, often spending the entire day chatting away like two old hens. We'd skip craft time inside to walk outside, and skip outdoor time to be crafty with each other inside. Although I grappled with the names of the nurses and sometimes forgot who the people in my framed photos were, I always felt witty and spry with Paul.

Then one day I visited Paul in his room. He sat on the edge of the bed, but wouldn't look at me.

"Vivian, I have something I need to confess."

My mind, dull as it can be these days, raced. Blanche Botish had her eye on him for weeks. Was he leaving me for that hussy? I promised I wouldn't cry or get angry.

"Well, get to your confession," I said with charm school poise.

"Vivian, you ought to know I'm part of a drug trial. I think it's the only thing I haven't told you."

I was so relieved I laughed at him. I thought my hip would break with the fit.

"You had me so worried, you fool. Don't you know we're all part of a drug trial here at Guinea Pig Acres?

Do you really think our kids pay for our entire upkeep? Merzer Pharmaceuticals pays the director here to have access to us. They only pretend to ask for our consent as part of the experiment - to see if hope plays a factor in their hocus pocus. In truth, the consent is written into the contract our kids sign to put us in here. They know the ungrateful little turds will never read the entire form. Some of us get placebos and some of us get something that may actually help. I figured everyone knew."

"Guess I spent too long sulking to notice."

"Well, now you know—" I tried to say his name, but the word vanished. A tear welled up in the corner of my eye. "If you don't mind, I think I'll go lay down now."

~ ~ ~

Paul noticed the fumble and the tear. Were they really all part of a science experiment? He watched to make sure Vivian went to the right room when she left to rest and it gave him hope that she didn't hesitate at any doors that weren't hers. Paul paced the empty hallways. Most everyone was on a tour to the art museum. He knew what he needed to do.

In the file room, Paul flipped through to the tab for C and saw his and Vivian's folders, his first, hers next, lying next to each other in the dark of a latched drawer. Paul shook off the image of them side by side in a morgue.

Just as he feared, Vivian was receiving a placebo. Mentally, Paul felt as good as ever and tested himself daily with lists of presidents, countries' capitals and state birds. He never once faltered. Although Paul knew what it would say, he checked his file - he was receiving the drug. He slammed the drawer and returned to the common room feeling heavy and lost.

The woman he loved was going to forget him, just as everyone else had done.

Paul fought for ideas. Break into the pharmacy? Give her half his dose? Give her all his dose? Switch her pills with someone else's? Why her? Why did it have to play out this way? What good were memories if you had no one to share them with? What good was love if it could be forgotten?

~ ~ ~

I feel so stupid. Paul. His name is Paul. Like the church in England, like the apostle, like the chipmunk-cheeked Beatle. Paul.

When he knocked on my door I didn't want to open it, but I did anyway. I wanted to see his face and feared the day I would forget his face. I didn't say anything, but the red contrasting his green eyes gave away that he'd been crying. He took me in his arms and squeezed me tighter than anyone has done as if he was holding on to keep from losing me.

"Come to my room," he whispered in my ear.

"We can do that in here."

"No, I need you to do something."

Intrigued, I followed him. He pointed to his stack of travel books.

"Where do you want to go?"

"How should I know? I've only ever been to Canada to fill a prescription."

"Anywhere," Paul urged. "You can go anywhere. Where will it be?"

I thought he was joking so I picked the first book my eyes landed on.

"Sicily."

"Get your things together. Whatever you can pack into two small bags."

"What's going on, Paul?" My heart skipped at the sound of my voice saying his name, at my mind remembering his name.

"Trust me?"

I couldn't resist that glittering spark in his eyes. I kissed him and rushed off to pack.

~ ~ ~

Paul's daughter never knew, but one account remained in his name. It started years ago as a college fund for Ella's brother. But when Edmund committed suicide at seventeen, the account was ignored. It had gained and lost, but mostly gained for over thirty years. When Ella told him of her plan to dump him in Century Acres, Paul cashed out the account worried that he might one day forget about its contents.

He knew what he was doing was crazy. He knew without the experimental meds he would forget, and Vivian was already heading down that road. But forgetting themselves on an island in the Mediterranean seemed a far better option than rotting away in Century Acres watching his new found love deteriorate while he remained healthy.

~ ~ ~

I'm running away with—with—oh, dear. Well, I'm running away with Mr. Cohen, at least I know that much.

~ ~ ~

The villagers adopted the Americans as Nonno and Nonna Cohen. At the old couple's request, the town artist drew their portraits, labeling each face with its name. The Swiss couple they rented from checked in daily to remind them to shop and eat, and the local children left flowers and lemons at their doorstep. Paul and Vivian enjoyed the sun, loved each other, and never looked back.

~ ~ ~

I can't remember the name of this little village. It's beautiful and the people treat us as if we're long lost relatives. Are we? I don't remember, but I don't remember this place either so perhaps they're new. I think I had children although the feeling isn't very strong. I suppose I would recall them if they cared for me like these villagers do.

I do know my feelings for the handsome man lying next to me. I stare at him each morning waiting for memories of our life together to kick in. He seems familiar, like someone I've always known, but I can only remember the past year. Perhaps that's all we've had.

I look over his shoulder. I don't know why, but it strikes me as a habit I need to keep up. Then, on his nightstand I see his portrait. Oh, yes.

"Good morning, Paul."

I know from the perplexed look on his face that overnight he's forgotten who I am too, but then he checks my nightstand and love jogs his memory.

"Hello, Vivian."

The Heron

When the Decemberists came out with their song "The Crane Wife," I was fascinated by the beautiful Japanese story of a man falling in love with a crane and her turning human to become his wife. Seeing that this could be retold as a magical, modern tale, "The Heron" was born. It's a tale of giving too much of yourself to be loved. This story won Honorable Mention from the Alabama Writers Conclave and from Writer's Journal magazine.

Looking over his shoulder, he discovered the truth. All her efforts, the sickness from exhaustion she endured, were they worth putting her through this? He wanted to say no, to be the kind of guy who put others first; instead he only hoped she could continue making him rich.

The dripping Northwest day filled with misting clouds bleeding through fabric to skin found Arno roaming Forest Park's weaving trails. He couldn't afford a rain jacket. With what they'd given him upon release he couldn't even afford a drink to loiter in the overheated confines of a coffee shop. The park's looming conifers offered some protection from the penetrating winter wet and the movement of walking warmed him just enough.

Rounding the bend along the portion of the Wildwood Trail that veered off to Pittock Mansion, he noticed a white, rain-sodden animal on the path. His eyes pushed through the haze to see the long legs and wisps of feathers. Inching forward he expected it to fly away, but it stayed; its beak gaping open then closed was the only motion. Open then closed like a stranded fish straining to breathe air as if fear of death could force spontaneous evolution. Approaching closer he detected a spot on the bird's breast with blood dribbling down into the mud. Half of her shined white, the other was muddy chocolate; the halves linked with a filament of blood.

He lifted the elegant bird. As it fixed a steady blue eye on him he marveled at the lightness of her. A flickering memory of high school biology class reminded him bird's bones were hollow, but he equated the weightlessness to her life slipping away. He wrapped her in his sweatshirt hoping the action wasn't a jailable offence. He couldn't risk another sentence so soon.

"Don't worry, Cole'll fix you." The bird stared at him before laying its curving neck down to nestle her head into the shirt.

"It's a BB." Cole's forceps dipped into the anesthetized bird's chest. "When'd you get out?"

Arno ignored the question. "How can you tell?"

"It's a common wound. Probably kids testing out their Christmas presents. Do you have money?"

"I got enough. Focus on her."

"I never took you for a bird lover."

"I don't even know what it is."

Cole looked at his brother. He never understood how one of them ended up in veterinary medicine and the other in petty crime. Arno was in a low patch, but he'd soon find some scam to bring himself back up. His brother the roller coaster.

"Even the worst ornithology student can identify a heron. The color is gorgeous though. Unusual."

"She'll be okay?" Arno asked.

Cole dropped the tiny metal ball into the tray. The ping echoed through the room.

"Why do you care? I'm surprised you didn't take it home for dinner."

"I run a few cons; I don't kill."

"It's just odd for you to care about something other than yourself."

"I just saw her there and—" He couldn't explain his concern. The bird was too beautiful not to love.

"I'll have to turn her over to Audubon for rehabilitation tomorrow morning."

"I can't keep her?"

"She needs to be in the wild."

Arno watched the bird's deep rhythmic breaths after Cole put her in the barred cage.

The phone woke him.

"You took her."

"Took who?" Arno said, trying to sound awake.

"Don't tell me you don't know. I knew you were desperate, but you said you'd never hit my place."

"What're you talking about?"

"The clinic was broken into last night. Only the bird is missing. You're going to tell me you have nothing to do with it?"

"Thanks for the trust, Cole." Arno snapped the phone shut.

Too irritated to go back to sleep, Arno dressed to go out. He knew who to question. Only a couple guys in town forged the permits and supplied the animals for Portland's lucrative exotic pet trade. He bolted out of the apartment building and papers went flying as a body slammed into his. He moved to shrug past. Whoever ran into him could get their own damn—

"Sorry, I'm such a klutz," the blonde woman said. His urgency vanished at the sight of her.

He stooped down, flustered by the switch from anger to lust. "No, my fault." He picked up the papers while she continued blaming herself.

"I wasn't paying attention. You really don't need to— Oh please, don't look at those," she pleaded as he looked at the drawings.

"You're an artist?"

"Trying to be." Her blush made her even more desirable. "I just flubbed another interview by being late."

"Do you want to have breakfast?" he blurted, certain she would say no. But she agreed and breakfast turned into a stroll leading back to his place where he kissed the round scar on her paper white breast as they made love.

Within a week Hera moved in. Although apologetic - video surveillance outside the building proved Arno's innocence - Cole believed his brother a fool. "She could rob you blind."

"She's worth the risk, besides don't you think I might be the worse influence."

Her drawings showed a detail and precision he'd never encountered. She could duplicate any image to the point where it was impossible to tell original from copy.

"Can you do money?" He handed her a twenty-dollar bill. "This perhaps?"

She gathered up her papers and pens and went to the bedroom.

"Where are you going?"

"You know I'm embarrassed to work in front of you." A gorgeous blush flashed over her cheeks.

"Why?"

"I don't know, but that's the rule if you need a counterfeiter."

"I didn't—" he started to protest.

"Hush," she kissed his lips. "You go out at all hours after muffled phone calls and come back looking like the cat who ate the canary. I don't mind. I'd like to help."

"Can you fool a bank?"

"Foreign currency would be better."

He turned and dug a twenty-euro note out of a drawer. "Like this?"

In less than an hour she emerged with five bills.

"Which is the real one?" Arno asked.

Hera shrugged coyly.

He couldn't tell the difference and neither could the banks.

Four bills an hour was her limit. Her exhaustion grew along with their stash, but he urged her on. Rather than produce more bills, she asked to copy a hundred-euro note instead, but he worried the large bill might draw notice. Arno sulked over her inability to work harder.

Every day behind the bedroom door she crafted a stack of money. Dark circles formed under her eyes and she could hardly eat from weariness. Her hair lost its glowing shine and she couldn't keep warm. Still, she never asked to quit and his greed became too insatiable to make the offer.

One day she shuffled into her room, sweater hanging loosely off her thinning frame. She failed to notice the door didn't latch. Passing by the mirror in the hall across from her work room, Arno caught his reflection. And hers. The temptation to watch her work was irresistible and he remained glancing at the reflection over his image's shoulder.

Her form shrank as if the sweater was swallowing her. He didn't trust his eyes and looked over his shoulder into the room. There it was. The brilliant white heron he found. Or was it? It looked similar, but this creature was a tattered patchwork of feathers like a dog with mange. The head bent down carefully as if fearing pain and plucked out a pile of feathers. The sweater formed again into human shape. Hera brushed one hand over a feather, each stroke transformed the feather a little bit at a time until it resembled the money she held in the other hand.

He stepped in. "How are you doing that?"

She stared at him, her mouth gaping as the bird's beak had done on that dripping day.

"I wanted to live that day you found me. You gave me what I wanted. I thought you loved me for what I was, not for my magic, and swore if I lived I'd give you what you wanted most," her voice rasped. "I thought you loved me, but you demand more and more. I fear I'll never make you happy."

She collapsed into her sweater, reverting into a half-feathered heron once more.

His throat clenched with emotion. He scooped up Hera and once again wrapped her in his jacket. He sped to Cole's.

"Help her, please."

Cole stared at the once beautiful bird.

"I'm so stupid. I believed you."

"What?"

"You broke in that night. You couldn't just do the right thing and let Audubon take her."

"I didn't."

"I suppose she walked out and followed you home."

"Help her."

Cole put the stethoscope to the bird's chest. The faint, off-kilter rhythm proved what he knew.

"She's dying. She's obviously been malnourished or stressed for some time. Her heart is giving out. Couldn't you figure out how to care for her, to give her what she needed? You ruined this beautiful thing."

Arno's head drooped. He knew.

"I'm turning you in. I trusted you all these years. Instead, you've screwed me over and killed her. You're worthless."

He knew.

Hera breathed once more, then her blue eyes faded.

Feeding Suspicions

"Feeding Suspicions" had been in my head for years after seeing how much mayo and butter my mom would put on my stepdad's sandwiches or toast. I thought of turning the idea into a novel, but there just wasn't enough complexity to the story – believe me, I tried. I gave it up for a couple years and then eventually had to get it out of my head. I eventually came up with this short story.

W hy won't he die? He deserves to die and the fact that he's still alive isn't for my lack of trying. I'll tell you one thing, once he goes I'm never marrying again. I've played the fool enough for one lifetime.

Michael and me. It's the same old story. We met each other and believed the circumstances much too fortuitous to be chance. It *had* to be destiny

Good lord, we took the same bus to work.

We commuted with fifteen other people at the same time everyday. Was it fate that we should meet them too? Of course not, but Michael and I believed the universe brought us together and our lives, our thoughts, our dreams and our hormones revolved around our Couple Kingdom for several months of infatuation.

We moved in together and once we discovered we could stand the sight of each other every morning, we planned to be married.

At the wedding Michael's mother cried over his dad missing the event. He'd been taken down by a heart attack days before he reached his fiftieth birthday, the same age Michael's grandfather died when he too was claimed by a bad ticker. My mom, never one to be subtle, pulled me aside at the reception with her eyes indiscreetly focused on Michael's mother and sister, both grossly overweight and both shoveling large scoops of cake into their mouths.

"You need to keep tabs on the weight of your new husband," she advised with scorn, "or he'll end up like one of them." On the final word she jerked a nod toward the nibbling, bulbous duo.

I, the glowing bride, rolled my eyes, "It won't happen, Mom. Michael watches what he eats and works out daily. He's quite buff." I cringe now remembering the pride in my voice.

"Regardless, you can never be too sure."

She shot another judgmental look across the room as Michael, carrying a plate mounded with cake, joined his mom and sister.

Despite my mom's prejudice against my husband's pudgy maternal side and cardiovascularly inferior paternal side, Michael and I were happy. We cavorted through the honeymoon stage for a couple years during which everything the other did was fascinating. I'd watch him shave and do the dishes; he'd watch me put on make up and fix dinner.

I can't say exactly when I noticed, but after a couple more years we'd gotten used to each other. My mascara application became a lonely affair, we did more things on our own that we once insisted on doing together and sometimes I didn't even know where in the house he was or bother finding him.

I took this as a normal part of marriage.

Until he started working late.

The flags instantly unfurled in my mind. That was the standard line, wasn't it? He was a network engineer, meaning he kept the computers for a multi-branch bank talking to each other, updated and virus-free. He didn't have a set office where I could, oh say, just happen to drop in and check up on him. My only contact was his cell phone. I rang with the pretense of being unable to find a screwdriver, to ask what he might want for dinner (often met with his response to not bother, he didn't know when he'd be home) or some other trivial matter that I hoped would remind him of me. Or at least distract him. My suspicion skyrocketed as my calls went straight to voice mail more and more often.

Out of habit, I read over Michael's pay stubs when I could find them. The more recent checks were larger than his old ones and recorded a good number of overtime hours so perhaps he wasn't lying about working late. Still, with all those cute female co-workers who understood his techie jargon and Star Trek jokes, his fishing off the company dock wasn't unimaginable.

Last year's holidays confirmed everything.

The week prior to Christmas as I sorted laundry – and yes, inspecting his shirts for lipstick stains and checking pockets for evidence – I found it. In his pants' pocket hid a piece of paper crimped tightly from his habit of folding any scrap in half as many times as possible. I pried the paper open, expecting a love letter or phone number, but instead revealed a receipt.

From a jewelry store.

And it wasn't a minor purchase.

Handwritten in enviably elegant script were the words: Nine-inch diamond bracelet. Paid in full. Cash.

At the bottom a bold outlined box emphasized the total: $1,264.

Had I been a cartoon character my eyes would have bulged out of my head two or three times as my tongue lolled out of my mouth. I didn't know what to make of it. Was this the reason for the late nights? This would be our fifth Christmas together. Perhaps he wanted to surprise me with something special. It was completely beyond what we could afford and I would have to insist he take it back, but the promise of his thoughtfulness forced me to cast aside the suspicions that had raged through me day and night for the past several months.

During the following week whenever I encountered a mirror I practiced my *you-shouldn't-have* and *I'm-so-surprised* faces. When five presents greeted me on Christmas morning, I pictured those feigned reflections in my mind. I tore through wrapping paper and yanked the top off the first four gift boxes hoping my searching and digging through tissue paper for the nine-inch diamond bracelet wasn't obvious.

Where was the damn thing?

Opening the last gift, a box too small to house a nine-inch diamond bracelet, the tissue revealed a pair of glittery butterfly earrings.

"Do you like them?" Michael had the nerve to ask.

Visualizing jabbing the posts on which those little insects perched into Michael's pupils, I forced a half-smile - nothing like the enthusiastic grins from the mirror - and hissed out a "Yes."

The rest of the day my mind raged. It was all I could do to not lash out over the clove-studded ham and bubbly scalloped potatoes. I ground the food in my mouth and swallowed without tasting a bite of the meal.

I knew the truth now.

What doubt could I have that he was cheating on me? I nit-picked through my recollection of the past few months and the signs glowed brighter than the Vegas Strip: his lack of attentiveness, the canceling of the detailed cell phone bill (which he said they were doing to save paper) and the increased infrequency of our lovemaking.

As I watched Michael eat egg rolls, deep-fried cheese and ranch dip at our New Year's Eve party, a certainty spelled itself out more plainly than a cake box recipe: I wanted Michael dead.

He deserved to die. Someone else was wearing my $1,264 nine-inch diamond bracelet and I didn't even merit a proper guilt gift from the jerk.

I took to the matter rationally. This wasn't going to be a crime of passion bash-him-over-the-head-with-a-lamp scenario. No, he made a fool of me and deserved everything coming to him.

Divorce wasn't an option. Not in my mind. Why should I embarrass myself and have people think I wasn't good enough, that I couldn't keep my husband in line? Why should someone else – the nine-inch diamond bracelet-wearing Wife Number Two - be subjected to this kind of treatment? Doesn't she realize he'll do the same to her as he did to me?

My plan? Simple. Kill him with food. No, not poison, I'm not a power hungry fourteenth century queen, and I'm not talking about foie-gras style force-feeding until his system overloads (tempting, but too messy).

No, all it would take was simple genetics, the human ability to pack on fat. And time. Not a problem; I'm a patient woman.

Before we married, Michael maintained a good level of fitness, but his increased hours and lack of motivation on the weekends already meant he was having a hard time keeping the scale on his good side. So far it didn't show through his clothes, but when he undressed his paunch puffed out like a soufflé.

The table was set for my payback.

Michael's weakness for all things porcine made breakfast an easy place to begin. Bacon started appearing regularly in the shopping cart and frying pan. His three eggs crackled in the residual fat and I used a heavy hand in the butter crock for his toast.

Healthy packed lunch? Not anymore. I bought the fattiest cuts of lunchmeat and painted a thick coat of mayo on both pieces of his sandwich bread. Potato chips, two candy bars instead of one, and a soda topped it off. The paper sack always returned home empty.

For dinner I made frequent use of the Fry-o-Lator – a wedding gift I thought I'd never have a use for. When veggies were present I ensured they swam in cream sauce or drowned under bleu cheese dressing.

I might as well have injected a pound of lard under his skin. Michael hefted on twenty pounds within a month and thirty more over the next two.

He tried to eat less, but the habit of indulgence was tightly seated. If I cut back the lunch snacks, he craved "a little something" and lumbered to the vending machine or mini-mart to purchase the lacking items with change I dropped into his lunch sack. When he'd ask for less mayo on his sandwiches I'd comply, but was sure to place butter and irresistible fresh rolls on the table at dinner.

By late April, he'd lost ten pounds, but gained seventy overall. Even resting, his breathing rasped in and out as if his whole system struggled to deliver oxygen to his bulk. The railing along the staircase started to pull loose as he used it more and more to pull himself up the stairs. Our already infrequent lovemaking came to a stop - he didn't have the energy for it. I didn't mind. The sight of the overhanging belly and dimpling on his rear were more than enough to put me out of whatever mood I fancied myself to be in.

May brought another ten pounds and a Northwest heat wave - a sudden jump from a chilly sixty degrees up to eighty-five. Michael's body, unaccustomed to the insulating weight gain, sprawled and flushed like a beached walrus. I saw him check his pulse a couple times and began to hope. Could the weather be the final ingredient to complete the deadly mix of a fat-laden diet and poor genetics?

I couldn't resist expediting the blend.

"It's nice out, we should go for a walk," I said.

"It's too hot," Michael mumbled from his shaded lawn chair.

I looked to the thermometer. The red climbed to eighty-two. "It's only seventy. C'mon, you keep saying you need to get some exercise. Let's go."

"Not today."

"You need to start somewhere," I said with a cheerleader's dose of enthusiasm.

His jowls quivered as he mumbled something else, but he hoisted himself out of the creaking chair. "Fine, I'll walk."

I marched him up every slope in our hilly neighborhood. Up and down for forty minutes in the heat of the day. I ignored his wheezing, ragged breath and chided him when he wanted to slow down. Finally he leaned over, hands on knees, to catch his breath.

"I don't feel well."

"Probably just thirsty," I stuck my water bottle out to him. "Here, have a sip."

He slurped from it and water dribbled down his chins. We finished the hill, and at the top came the sign I'd been waiting months for: Michael rubbing and shaking his arm. I let him go home to rest.

After a few minutes of lying on the couch he bolted upright clutching his chest.

"Call 911," he grunted.

I tried to act worried. I'd gotten good at acting over the past months. Acting like I cared for him, like I didn't want him dead, like I wasn't counting the minutes to my freedom from the cheating bastard.

"Are you sure? It's not just indigestion, is it?"

His face contorted, "I'm sure. Call."

I pulled out my cell phone and dialed a nine, a one, and then a two. I placed the phone to my ear and waited a few seconds.

"Ambulance," I paused. "My husband's having a heart attack." Pause. I gave our address. Pause. "Okay." Longer pause as I nodded my head at the non-existent words on the other end of the line. "Please hurry." I closed the phone.

"It'll be ten minutes. You going to be okay until then?"

He breathed in as deep as he could, "I think so, just scary, you know?"

Minutes ticked by. Michael grew paler. He grunted, groaned and squealed in worried pain, but said he'd be okay if the ambulance got there soon. I played my part by pacing the front room, checking out the window, opening the door to look and listen for help that wasn't coming, all the while mentally chanting: "Why won't he die?"

Fifteen minutes later, Michael started drifting, his breathing gurgled, and his face paled to gray. It would be over soon. I held back my grin.

"I'm not going to make it," he whispered. "How long has it been?"

"Only seven minutes - just hold out a little longer."

"No, it's too late. I want to tell you something before I go."

So, he needed to clear his conscience before the big goodbye. Fine. Whatever. It didn't absolve him.

"Go on."

"In my closet, you know that box I keep the postcards in?"

I nodded. He saved postcards in an old shoebox from all our trips together, even weekend getaways to the beach. The memory made my throat tighten and I hated myself for the emotion.

"There's another box inside. I bought it for you last Christmas. Saved up," he gasped as new pain coursed through him. "I wanted to give you something you'd never get yourself. I chickened out. Worried you'd be mad I spent so much. Silly, huh? Bust my butt all those extra hours and then not give it to you. You deserve so much. You're so good to me. I love you."

He stopped breathing. Just like that, no theatrics, just gone.

I went to the closet. What had he meant about giving me something? He couldn't mean—

I slid the postcard box out from under a photo album. My hands shook as I lifted off the lid.

Oh no. No—

The box of postcards fell from my grasp spilling our memories onto the carpet.

Lying among them was a long black case.

Oh, Michael. Tears dripped off my face as I bent to pick it up.

I opened the case.

My heart stopped then pounded back into rhythm.

There it was.

The nine-inch diamond bracelet.

My body, no longer able to hold its own weight, crumpled to the floor.

What had I done?

Desmond, Casey and the Stonemason

Another contest-inspired story during my Everything-Italian phase. For anyone curious, in ancient Rome it was illegal to put a Vestal Virgin to death because spilling their blood might offend the gods. Instead, Vestal Virgins who committed crimes such as losing their virginity or letting the city's eternal flame go out were punished by being buried alive with a hunk of bread and a little water. This way, their "fate" was in the hands of the gods. I doubt whether there were actual Vestal Locks, but I do feel Desmond's pain of walking miles and miles through Roman museums and just wanting to find the bar.

T he $500,000 invoice sent his stomach fluttering, but only for a moment. Regardless of his wealth, Desmond never could rid himself of this poor-boy reaction to the cost of his whims. But within seconds, a Seven Deadly Sins brand of pride replaced the plummeting *can-I-afford-this* sensation. The money could have sent thousands of kids to college, it could have fed the poor, it could have purchased land for the Nature Conservancy. Desmond smirked while swiping his card through the reader, then stifled a giggle as he entered his PIN and accepted the transaction. All those noble causes screwed over for this thing that would be buried six feet under.

It was no ordinary casket. No, what stood before him was a work of art he'd wanted since last year's annual trip to Italy.

In Rome, all he cared to do was sip wine at the *enoteca* and watch the *cameriera* swish between tables, but Casey dragged him off to the Capitoline Museum - two buildings, underground passages, innumerable busts of old men and a wife who had to see everything. And, since Casey was too absorbed to translate the visitors' guide, Desmond couldn't make heads or tails of where the museum's bar was. So he followed her from one dark room to the next, rolling his eyes at every coin and wondering how anyone could find this stuff interesting.

Then he saw one. Once he noticed it, he realized they lined the entire room.

"What are those?"

"Sarcophagi. Didn't you see the others?"

"Others?"

"Well, these are nice, but we need to go back towards the entrance to see the best."

"More walking?"

"I'll walk a hundred miles if you're actually interested in something here."

The walk was worth every step. Carved into an eight-foot marble box raged a battle scene as detailed as a photo taken the moment of the action.

"I've got to get one of those."

"Let's go grab a bite at the bar."

"I'll meet you there," Desmond said, taking in every grimace, every spear jab, every terrified enemy. Yes, he had to have one.

Upon returning from Italy, Desmond ordered Casey to get him in touch with the best stonemason in New York.

"I'd prefer if you asked me nicely." Casey tapped on her phone's screen. Her position as curator at MOMA kept her in contact with the nation's top restoration artists.

"Are you going to get me my artist, or what?"

"What's this about? You hate art. Sometimes I think you hate me because I enjoy art." She smiled at something on the screen.

"Is this tirade going to take long? I'm sure my secretary could do this without the attitude."

"Don't bother her." Desmond's phone pinged. "I just sent you the information."

~ ~ ~

The stonemason could only stare as Desmond described the scene he dreamt up on the flight home.

"The marble alone will cost tens of thousands," said the stonemason. "And I don't work cheap."

"Do you think I can't pay?" Desmond swung his arm in a game show host's flourish, inviting him to observe the handmade Italian furniture, the artwork the Louvre borrowed on occasion, the crystal chandelier handcrafted at Waterford. All contained within the entire top floor of the Manhattan skyscraper Desmond owned.

"I've no doubt you have the money, but you realize this thing's going into the ground, don't you?"

"Are you saying you don't want the job?"

"You haven't mentioned my salary."

"How long will it take you?"

"For this size and detail, about a year."

"Well, what's twelve months of your life worth? Double that number and cancel any plans because you're mine for the next year."

"What's the rush? Think you're dying or something?"

"Do you think I got where I am without planning for the future? You could learn a thing or two from me."

~ ~ ~

"He really said that?" Casey lay in the stonemason's arms as he traced circles over her bare belly. "He got where he is by stepping on people's toes, being cruel, breaking laws and killing puppies."

"Killing puppies?"

"I wouldn't put it past him."

"Leave him. Be with me."

"You know I would, but the damn pre-nup. Why did I ever trust him? If I leave I'm required to pay him back for every unwanted gift he's given me - and I'm sure he kept the receipts – plus I'm obligated to buy out half of that gaudy condo. I'd go bankrupt."

"But if he met with an accident?"

"What are you saying?"

"How well do you know Desmond?"

"Too well, why?"

"Will he want to try out his new toy?"

"He goes on nonstop, imagining what it'll be like to be inside, how stately he'll look, how impressed people will be. But couldn't he just kick off the lid?"

"Remember when you requested I study the Vestal Locks?"

"You figured them out?"

The stonemason nodded.

~ ~ ~

Designed by the Romans from a Greek idea, the trip latches known in archeological circles as Vestal Locks were used to imprison Vestal Virgins who broke their vows of chastity. By Roman law, no one could kill the priestesses of Vesta so the condemned were placed, while still alive, in sarcophagi. The victim entered on her own accord and, once she guided the lid into place, locks sprung shut. Her blood would therefore be on no one's hands if the gods happened to starve her to death. Only the person who created the box knew the location of the release mechanism to retrieve the body.

~ ~ ~

A year later, an invoice rested on top of Desmond's sarcophagus. He examined the carving before touching the paper. If he didn't like the work he could walk away. A loophole in the contract demanded complete satisfaction or the stonemason received nothing. Casey screeched her head off when she learned about that clause.

But the work was good. The scenes were exactly as he imagined: the glorious Desmond dressed as Zeus with his business rivals begging for mercy, another panel with him dressed as a commander of legions driving a chariot that crushed adversaries resembling the bleeding hearts who taxed the hell out of his profits, and another scene filled with naked women clamoring over one another to get to the Desmond Apollo who brandished a lightning bolt to symbolize his potency.

Desmond stepped onto the stool to examine his effigy. The lid of the sarcophagus bore a wrinkle- and jowl-free image of his face appearing more benevolent than it ever had in real life. The body was carved to resemble a lightweight silk tunic draped over a muscular body Desmond had never attained.

"I love it," he said as flipped over the invoice. The flutter, then the arrogant pride swept over him. This was barely a month's salary.

"Those poles though," he indicated two poles extending from either end of the lid, "none of the ones I saw had poles."

"They make it easier to slide the lid aside. Marble plugs hide the holes once the poles are removed."

"Fine, you get paid." Desmond swiped his card, entered his PIN and accepted the charge.

"Try it out," Casey suggested.

"Always putting me one step closer to the grave, right Casey? Do you think she'll be able to move it if we do most of the work? Weaker sex and all," Desmond elbowed the stonemason and gave a knowing wink.

"Only one way to find out," the stonemason said. "On the count of three you and I will move the lid to the side. Casey, you watch your end stays balanced. One. Two. Three."

Desmond strained to heave the marble lid. With the lid angled aside, the stonemason said, "Okay, Desmond, don't release before I say so or your effigy will shatter." He reached to Desmond's pole. "Alright."

"Are you sure you can handle the weight?" Desmond strained.

"Quite sure."

Desmond let go and the stonemason grunted with the extra weight, but soon settled into the effort.

"Kind of creepy, eh?" Desmond joked as he climbed into the cool interior. "Slide the lid shut. I want the full effect."

"Are you sure?" Casey asked.

"Don't question me, woman. Let me enjoy a minute of peace and quiet."

Casey looked to the stonemason. He gave a slight grin and a nod, then pushed the lid into position.

After a *click* he thought came from the lid fitting into place, Desmond lay in silence. The marble interior sucked the heat from him.

"Hope you guys are warm. I'm freezing in here," he laughed. "The icy hand of death and all that, eh?"

On the outside of the coffin they couldn't hear the joke.

"What do you think he's thinking?" the stonemason asked.

"Does it matter?"

The stonemason checked something on his phone.

"Not really, the transaction went through."

The marble muted sound from within and without. Casey and the stonemason couldn't hear Desmond screams to be let out. Nor could Desmond hear the poles being removed, the holes plugged and the studio being locked as Casey and the stonemason walked out hand in hand.

Part Three

EVENING

The Weaver

"The Weaver" is a strange tale. I don't really believe there are little workers weaving our strands of fate, but I like the idea of it and how it might work – especially with cocky new hires trying to show up their superiors. This is probably one of the quickest stories I've written - the entire thing popped into my head and got put down on paper in an hour while waiting for my car's oil to be changed. For reference, I imagined the mentor the Rookie is constantly thinking of as the Vincent Price character from the movie Edward Scissorhands.

"G ot it?"

"I think so."

"There's no 'I think so.' Either yes or no. People's lives are at stake. So, once again, got it?"

"Yes," I say making no attempt to hide my irritation.

"I'm giving you an easy one to start. This is the first you've woven on your own, right?"

"Yes sir."

"You remember how to do a simple braid?"

"Three strands over-under-over-under." I picture my mentor's hands whirring away on a simple braid to demonstrate mastery at the skill. His students, including myself, eventually wove the braid smoothly under his tutelage, but never with such speed. Still, there are limits to how fast you can braid a life.

"Brilliant, Rookie," the Head Knower says with a roll of his eyes. "This is straight-forward, no strange twists or additions. A dullard's life even you can handle. Here're the strands."

"Thank you, sir." I take the silvery filaments from his hand and he's right, this one will be simple. I hear my mentor reciting *The Fate Weaver's Tome of Instruction*:

"You can judge the complexity of what you'll be weaving from the initial contact with the strands. Their weight is in direct correlation to the life's twists and turns."

The demo strand we'd passed around class carried so much weight that, when looped over my finger, the digit began to turn white before I handed the piece on to the next apprentice. The strands my Knower has assigned me weigh next to nothing. It will be boring work, but I still need to be mindful of tearing, stretching, or breaking the strands. *The Tome* tells us not to let the weight of the strands fool us. Even though the person's life may be dull in the Weaver's opinion, it is still someone's life and not to be taken lightly. This dullard's Fate Strands will be woven as carefully as those making up a world leader or inventor. I mentally recite the First Rule of Weaving from my mentor's initial lesson.

"Rule One," he would say in his trilling voice, "says Weavers must not judge. We must simply bring the Strands of Fate together so the lives go on as the Knowers have seen."

These words play over and over in my mind as I work on my first strands. I didn't expect to be handed anything exciting for my first true weaving, but this is beyond dull. I struggle with the question of how someone can let his life be so plain. As my fingers move down the strand, I see his life going by and him not taking advantage of the gift. He does the least possible in school, he takes the easiest job that comes his way, never marries or forms any influential friendships and I'm certain his death will be of old age and natural causes.

I sigh as I braid in the filaments of a few acquaintances and mesh his work strand in for a good portion of his life, but I contain my boredom. The temptation is to snip off a bit of a tsunami strand and throw a challenge in for the guy, but the Knower didn't see that for him. I braid the filaments I've been given and tell myself over and over to treat it with care, to weave the glinting strands of life events together as if this person matters, which I know he doesn't. I could snap this person's strand in the middle, ending his life at forty instead of seventy-five and no one would care. But then I would be falling into the George Bailey Fallacy (renamed from the Dullard's Fallacy after the release of *It's a Wonderful Life* - required viewing for Weavers as it is the closest humans have gotten to understanding our work).

The Tome describes the Fallacy in this way: We tend to think because a person is dull, his or her life doesn't matter, but it does. They all do.

My mentor put it like this, "In essence, everyone's life affects someone else's at some point either greatly or minutely, for good or for evil, and that affect guides the affected from then on. It is not up to the Weaver to determine. That is the realm of the Knower."

So, the dullard I'm forcing myself to take care with might help a pregnant lady across the street who will give birth to someone important. The woman may or may not have been in danger, but the kindness of his act will somehow influence her and her child. You can't know what other Weavers are working on for this very reason. This is Rule Two (at least this person's dull life is giving me plenty of time to remember my training even if I'm not making the best use of it).

"Rule Two of *The Tome*," my mentor would say with haughty authority, "tells us one Weaver may not know another Weaver's work."

The rule is a check system to keep Weavers from making judgments about a life and "accidentally" snipping off a strand to prevent a chain of events (say Hitler's mom and dad meeting) or to "force weave" two lives together that never fully join (such as two friends a Weaver may want to see become lovers).

The temptations with what we could do with the strands we've been given are bad enough, but to be able to consult with other Weavers and see how our strands interact would make this temptation even greater. It would give us too much power. That power is left for the Knowers.

My first life ends as dully as I had expected. As the Head Knower appears by my side, I twist and tie off the braid thereby sealing off the life.

"All done?"

"You should know," I quip. The Knowers know (hence the name) just how long it should take even a rookie to weave their strands – approximately two weaving minutes per year of life. My Knower knew this one would take me about two and a half hours for the man's seventy-five years.

"That joke is old, Rookie." He holds out his hand for my strand. "But you kept to the expected time, pretty good for a first try."

"Thank you, sir." I hand over the shining braid.

He examines my simple project with an intensity I find a little silly. I know our tasks are important, but some Knowers take it a bit too seriously. I mean, they're *Knowers*, implying they should *know* what will happen, right? Not really, it's an easy to assumption to make. Knowers foresee a person's life through the end when they first touch a Fate Strand. They know which other pieces to grab for the Weaver to assemble the life, but Knowers cannot bring the strands together. *The Tome* calls this the Circular Conundrum: Do Knowers need Weavers or do Weavers need Knowers? My mentor's pride in being a Weaver burned bright whenever he presented this lecture:

"Knowers are powerful, that is to be certain, but they aren't allowed the knowledge of Weaving to prevent too much power from resting in any one set of hands. If Knowers saw the life and the outcomes of that life it would be too easy to change it. [Again he would regale with the Hitler Strand Example – what Knower wouldn't have crimped that strand early on?] Weavers are given the strands that go together. Our nimble fingers run down the Fate Strand for each life sensing moments the Knower's fingers cannot. The Knowers can't sense where to add in the strands of work, love or accidents they provide us. Knowers may see the life, but we as skilled Weavers bring the lives together."

We can also screw up. One mistake, say a fingernail catching and snagging a strand can change the course of that life. Pulling too hard and breaking a strand will instantly end a life. Weaving a side strand in at the wrong moment may result in missed opportunities. Two people meant to meet as young adults will not have the same interaction if they meet as six-year olds or sixty-year olds. Our strict adherence to detail and focused attention is bred into a Weaver along with the delicate finger sensitivity.

"It's good. Just as I saw." He puts away the braid, then passes me a new Fate Strand with a packet of smaller filaments. "Here's a harder one. Don't mess it up."

This strand tests more heavily against my fingers, but not much more than the previous. Caressing the tops of the others in the packet, flashes come into my mind and I can see the weight of the main Fate Strand will come from the influence of these side strands. In other words, left to her own devices this person would be as dull as the previous, but people and places will add to her life and she is willing to be guided by these influences in a way my first never would have been. Weight signifies neither good nor bad for us, it is simply a measure of the complexity of the braid at the end. This one will require more than a strand-over-strand weave. Her influences should mesh together like weaving of a piece of fabric.

I move my fingers down as the child grows from girl to woman. I then pull other strands from the packet and weave them in at the right moments. My interest in this one peaks higher, but my mind still drifts somewhat to my mentor and his lecture on how Weavers can do their job with such precision. He instilled in me a sense of pride in my actions.

"How is it we Weavers know just how and just so?" I can hear his rhetorical question as if he said it yesterday. "Our work is complex on a scale no other of the Fate Workers will understand. But it is also simple once you learn to trust your own fingers. The Fate Strands are formed in the Knower's mind during the mother's pregnancy. A Weaver's first touch is baby's first breath and as one hand, the Guiding Hand, moves down it reads the person's every moment ensuring the life follows the course set out for it. Our other hand, the one we call the Intuitive Hand, hovers over the string at a later point in the life than the Guiding Hand. The Intuitive Hand almost touches, but not quite. When a new piece is needed to be braided in, there is a blackness in the life story. This is where our work is so crucial. If the proper strand isn't woven in at the precise moment it is needed, the person of the main fate line will feel this emptiness we see as black, a feeling like they are missing out on something or that their life is incomplete. Conversely, put in any strand too early and the person feels as if they are in over their head; too late and opportunities may pass by. The teaching I will give you will train your fingers to detect these moments of black with delicate precision. Remember, the Knowers see lives as they should be, but only Weavers have the responsibility and skill to make it happen."

I smile to myself as I picture my mentor's hands flourishing in the air with this lecture. My second Fate

Strand comes together smoothly and the woman's life leads its course. I tie it off as the Knower returns to inspect my work yet again. I hold it out to him before he even reaches my station.

"Think you're pretty good, don't you?"

"Top of my class, sir."

"School is merely practice, Rookie. Rehashing dead people's strands isn't anything like working with the real thing."

I bristle at the insult to my training and my mentor.

"No, sir, but I am doing rather well for a first day. Even you have to admit that."

"Yes, I have to agree your work is impressive. No loose pieces like most rookies. All your lines are tightly woven and well timed. Feel up for a challenge?"

"Without a doubt, sir."

"Here it is. No mistakes."

"Rule Three – Each strand is vital."

"This one especially so."

I begin to weave with my fingers gliding over the filament. The thought of how easily these shining hair-thin strands can be broken is never far from my mind. Too much pressure will snap the piece. It's a thought that eliminates some apprentice weavers; they find themselves unable to accept the responsibility of working with something so fragile yet so important, thus rendering their hands impotent.

The pieces fit together well and I can see this woman's world taking shape. A natural leader, excellent student and her ambitions will be achieved without hurting others in the process. A moral standard becomes ingrained in her fabric as I weave it – environmentally aware, culturally intelligent, repelled by violence – and when she wins her home state's senator seat I can't resist the temptation *The Tome* strictly warns against.

My mentor lectured us on this temptation repeatedly. Because the implications of seeing a life's ending are hard on the Weaver, it is strictly advised against. We know our strands will be tied off in the end, much as a farmer knows his prize pig will be up for slaughter one day, but it doesn't make the separation any easier. We all want our braids to be tied off peacefully. We are not meant to be involved. Seeing the future of a life, beyond reading for the black moments, is a recipe for involvement. It is akin to stepping into the realm of the Knowers.

But with this one I can't help it. This woman is so magnificent and interesting that I can't wait the few minutes it will take me to weave down her future. I feel like a human who can't resist reading the end of a book mid-way through the story.

When I see the woman's future, I smile for her and for myself. Pride surges through me for no reason except that my weaving will make it happen. The woman becomes a world leader, an example to other nations. I move my fingers down a bit more hoping to see the changes she enacts, to see the species her work will save, to see the world at peace. If anyone could do it, it's this woman.

Instead, I see the fear on her face as a car plows into her. Her strand grows thin after this. The signal of a slow, painful death.

I can't let this happen. Her life according to the Knower is written to end early, but my mentor instilled in me the confidence that Weavers are in full control. We can change outcomes. She needs to make the world better; she needs to live.

I take the strand of the other driver and weave it in a moment sooner than it should be. The driver will hit a telephone pole instead of my woman's car. She will see the accident and be thankful for the timing of it, knowing that had it happened a moment later she would have been killed. My fingers move down and the only affect of the accident is to hold her up in traffic for an hour as they clear the damage.

I quickly weave my way along. The Knower will be coming soon since, according to his calculations, the braid should be ending in only a few moments. If I can get her to begin the work I want her to do, he can't unravel it. Rule Four: What is woven cannot be changed.

Unfortunately, my fingers aren't quick enough as I stumble over the side strands I have available. My Knower rushes over to me and yanks my braid away. He snaps the end. Her life is over. Even Knowers can manage that much.

"What are you doing?" we yell simultaneously.

We stare at each other, glaring as if the fury can undo what the other has done and force out an answer.

"You could have ruined everything," he grumbles.

"You *did* ruin everything," I shout. Other Weavers glance up but then go immediately back to work knowing any mistake will be punished tenfold at the moment.

"Rookie Weavers. Idiots. I should have never trusted you with this. You'll be weaving deadbeats the rest of your career."

"She had work to do."

"You think you know better than me?"

"I know she shouldn't die. She would have changed the world."

"Her death was the best thing for the world."

"Why? So humans can continue with corruption and destruction?"

"Her death was necessary to stop that. Do you think it's all haphazard what the Knowers do? I know you're trained to think Weavers are the end all and be all of existence, but you're not. Knowers have plans, we see more than one life at a time unlike you. We *know*."

"How can her death be necessary? Her work hadn't yet begun."

"Power was corrupting her already. That car trip was to make a deal with the worst of the agribusiness conglomerates to allow a lapse in regulations and environmental laws in exchange for campaign financing. Allowed freedom from overseers, their genetically dysfunctional seeds and poisons would have destroyed crops, fields, water supplies and ecosystems for generations; large-scale famine would be guaranteed. No one knew of this deal except them and her. Everyone else saw her as you did - perfect and promising. The accident you wove and the resulting traffic jam slowed her enough to prevent this meeting, but had she been allowed to live her corruption would eventually have undone everything you were hoping for."

"And her death?" I'm still fuming.

"Her death will become a rallying point for liberals *and* conservatives the world over. Her charm and likeability won her many allies. These allies will continue what she *said* she stood for. They are the ones who will make the changes you wanted her to make. She never would have accomplished anything on her own."

His statement forces the realization of my own arrogance. An arrogance that lead to disobedience and nearly undid all that my weaving hoped to accomplish. I had overstepped my bounds.

"I apologize."

"You'll be weaving meaningless lives from now on, you realize that don't you?"

"Yes."

"It's a shame. I saw great things coming from you."

I hang my head, too embarrassed to meet his eye. As my mentor said, Weavers make the life – even their own – and what I had woven could not be undone.

Apple

"Apple" is a melancholy post-apocalyptic story inspired by a first line contest, a long run of abnormally cold springs in the Northwest and having just read The Road *by Cormac McCarthy. The Doc's actions seem cruel, but he's practical since having children when you can't provide them food is never a good idea. This story won Second Prize in the Mary Mackey Short Fiction competition.*

The road wasn't on the map, but that didn't stop The Doc from looking anyway. He rotated the map until the arrow with the **N** pointed in the direction he felt certain was north and traced his finger along the route they'd traveled. No matter how tightly he squinted, this road just wasn't there. As he tried to work out how they'd lost the charted road, Amy shuffled around kicking at pebbles.

"I'm pregnant," she said as if telling one of the little stones she was thirsty.

The Doc's fingers clutched the map and he urged himself to relax. He couldn't tear the map. Who knew if they'd find another.

She couldn't be pregnant. Not now. Someday maybe, but not when they barely had enough food for one person let alone three. Sure, they'd been making love with a desperate frequency out of boredom, a need to stay warm and the simple comfort of being naked together, but with so much death he hadn't dreamed she, or anyone, could harbor new life.

He relaxed his grimace and looked up from the map to Amy's hollow face. He recalled how he winced when her hips ground into his during last night's sloth-slow intimacy. He remembered the sense of loss and helplessness when the flanged bone of her pelvis, covered only by a hint of skin, jutted into his.

They were starving and another mouth would make it worse.

Supposing, of course, they survived another nine months.

But she couldn't be.

"Are you certain?"

"Yeah. How could I not know?"

How could she not? He pondered back to the last embarrassing time when, for lack of any feminine hygiene products, she tore up a t-shirt to catch the flow. Of how, even then, her underwear was so loose on her wasting frame the elastic couldn't hold the t-shirt shreds tight enough and blood dribbled down her leg. That had been so long ago. Or had it? Through the hunger, he couldn't keep track of time. Survival after The Disaster he could handle. Keeping track of time? No. The red-legged incident could have been last month or even three months ago. What he did know is since that occasion, she hadn't torn up any more shirts.

"When was your last period?"

"I dunno. A couple months ago. I didn't say anything the first month, but I missed it again. You know how regular I am."

Oh yes, the half moon. Her period always came at the half moon. He noted to himself that using the moon as a way to keep time would be a good idea. It was so regular, so unaffected by Earth. Even if the Earth's gravity held it, the moon had more effect on the planet than the planet did on its cratered satellite. His gut grumbled and the thought floated away.

"We need to turn around. This road's not on the map and I don't want to get lost."

"Why? Even if where we're going is on the map, it's not as if anything's going to be there."

"We don't know that. Besides, it makes me feel better knowing we're on the road to somewhere. Does that make sense?"

"Yeah."

"And old houses and stores appear more frequently on mapped roads. We need to find more food. You need to eat more if you think you're pregnant."

She stopped trailing by his side.

"You don't think I am. Just because you used to be a doctor—"

"I am a doctor," he said more harshly than he intended. His hunger magnified every irritant. Knowing they had to retrace their path grated him like a jagged piece of glass coated in lemon juice grinding into his foot's sole.

"If there are no hospitals, then you're only trained in medicine. Plus, you were only a naturopath, not a *real* doctor."

This used to be joke between them back when they joked with each other, back when their world didn't feel covered in heavy clouds. He knew it was time to stop talking. They didn't have the energy to waste on arguing, but the no-longer joke scratched at his nerves.

"I believe you've gone into amenorrhea. You've lost too much body fat for your uterus to waste resources prepping for a baby."

"So you don't think I'm pregnant."

The words sounded so stupid he wanted to walk away and leave her to her own devices on this damn uncharted road. But he remained civil. They could get back to the main road by dusk if they turned around now. And there'd been an apple tree just as they turned onto this road. At mid-summer, the apples wouldn't be quite ripe, but they'd be edible. He knew they needed fat, but any calories would do. They needed to get moving.

"I think it's unlikely," he took her hand, "but not impossible."

Her smile took hostage of her bone and skin face. He wondered how she could want to bring a baby into a world where they scavenged and starved every day. A world where even unripe apples seemed like Thanksgiving.

~ ~ ~

The Disaster had been bad. Still, with seven billion people on the planet, there'd been enough survivors to continue. Electricity was non-existent, but human power was enough to turn fields and plant crops. For Amy and The Doc, as The Community began to call him, it had been almost idyllic until the final few years. Things turned a wrong corner and crops wouldn't grow in The Community's gardens. The climate shifted making it too cold and too wet for too long for warm-weather crops to thrive. And cold-weather crops struggled as if something in the soil strangled the life out of the leaves and shoots. Without external sources of food, The Community starved, buried their dead and hoped next year would be better.

When a third May in a row started out cold and wet, The Doc knew it was time to go. He and Amy packed what they could into backpacks and panniers and left on their bicycles. The Doc kept their direction always south and always east. He hoped down there it might be better - warmer with a longer growing season. After the years of increasingly colder Northwest weather, a hot humid southern summer sounded like perfection.

They scavenged and did well with the little camp stove he'd bought back when it was a cozy and quaint to be without electricity during a winter storm. The few people they encountered were wary but friendly, always willing to point on his map where they were. They'd been making good time until a group of men stole the bikes. The Doc was thankful they didn't seem interested in Amy's emaciated body, but he regretted the loss of the stove he'd stashed in the panniers. Hot water, a meager soup of leaves, even just a light in the dark all went with the stove.

He'd done well so far, never making them retrace their steps until now. This going back seemed like bad luck and he realized he'd grown superstitious since losing the stove. Two birds meant a bad day (there'd been two birds the morning they lost the bikes). A fallen limb pointing northwest meant someone else from The Community had died. He yearned to give meaning to things. This morning he'd seen two birds and now Amy had dropped her bombshell.

With a crack and crash, a limb fell from a poplar and three bluebirds flew from the undergrowth. It had to mean something.

"Wait here," he told her before jogging over to the branch. The tip of the fallen branch pointed to a clump of an herb The Doc knew well. Ingesting a few leaves of the plant caused miscarriage. He looked to Amy and his mind ran a marathon of thoughts. Could she be pregnant? Perhaps there was a reason they'd gone this way. Perhaps this was why, after so long of not getting lost, he turned down this road. This was no world for babies. Not yet anyway. The Doc stooped to pluck some of the leaves. An hour later, he and Amy munched on a supper of apples.

~ ~ ~

As they walked with the sun fading behind them, Amy's stomach rumbled and he handed her the leaves.

"Chew on these, they'll dull the hunger."

She took them, smelled them, then popped them in her mouth and chewed the leaves like gum. He took her hand and they kept walking.

That night, when her stomach cramped and ached, he rubbed her belly to soothe it.

"Too many apples, I guess," she grunted.

"Perhaps."

"I'll name the baby Apple if it's a girl."

He swallowed back the emotion her hopefulness swelled in him and continued rubbing her concave belly.

"That'd be a good name."

The Toad

"*The Toad*" *is a modern re-telling of a medieval Italian folk tale. In it, the very ugly Bertoldo is jester to the king and becomes one of the king's best friends and truest advisors. Feeling others are viewing the king as being controlled by Bertoldo and embarrassed by her husband's friendship with the hideous jester, the queen takes matters into her own hands to get Bertoldo out of their lives. Some of the exchanges between Bert and Albert are close translations of the Italian text.*

~ 1 ~

"Albert, did you hear that?"

"No, I'm sleeping."

"I heard something."

"Probably just the cat. Sleep. Now."

Albert tried to return to his dream, but the creaking of the pantry door jolted him to full alert. He jumped out of bed and grabbed the largest and nearest item to him.

"Are you going to defend your kingdom with an umbrella?" Miriam chided.

"Don't wake me up just to criticize."

With the alligator leather strap holding it closed and its pointed metal tip, the umbrella made a perfect impromptu sword in Albert's opinion. Besides, for two hundred dollars it ought to serve double use as something.

Albert tiptoed out from the bedroom knowing where to step to keep the floorboards from squeaking. It was the same route he took toward the stairs to his study on the first floor where he would call his mistress at any hour. Sheila would have never criticized his choice of weaponry.

The pantry door creaked shut while Albert crept his way down the stairs. The clang of pots and pain-ridden "oof" signaled Albert to sweep in and take the burglar (who would now be rubbing his head) by surprise. Albert knew all too well the thief had just crashed into the array of copper pots and pans hanging above the center island in the kitchen.

Miriam, after seeing the "kitchen of her dreams" in a *Better Homes and Gardens*, insisted they remodel the kitchen she never used, complete with pots and pans hanging dangerously at the level of Albert's head. Since completion of the remodel, the cookware hadn't been moved except by Albert's head. Their personal chef preferred cast iron pans, but Miriam demanded they be kept out of sight, and so the only use for the dangling metal was to give the maid something else to dust and an obstacle for Albert to watch out for.

"Gotcha," Albert jutted the umbrella forward as he burst through the kitchen door like a pajama-wearing Errol Flynn.

"Got me? What, am I going to have to witness your Mr. Steed impersonation? Only if Emma Peel shows up, Old Man."

Albert was flustered. Who was this ugly little man to talk back to him? No one ever talked back to him. He was Albert Pearl, head of Pearl Enterprises. He controlled more things than he could keep track of. So who did this guy think he was?

"I'll have you know there is a security system on this house and the police will be arriving any minute." Because if they didn't the Chief knew Albert would arrange to have him replaced.

"Oh, you mean this?" The strange man held up a couple wires. "You got robbed on your security system. Any thief worth his salt can get through it. You've obviously got the cash, you should really invest in better things."

"I was told it was the best on the market," Albert lowered the umbrella.

"Most expensive on the market, but not the best. You ought to do some research before plunking down your dough."

Albert snapped to his senses. Why was he bothering with this little worm? This was no time for conversation. He aimed the weapon again.

"Put down that bag. You won't steal anything from me."

"Oh yeah, god forbid you not have," he glanced around, "well, everything from the looks of it."

"I've earned what I have. Can you say the same?"

"I've earned my reputation that's for sure. And what sort of reputation do you have, I wonder."

"The bag," Albert gestured a lowering motion with the umbrella tip.

The man with the crooked nose and even more crooked teeth pushed the messenger bag toward Albert who bore a perfectly straight nose and wore teeth made straight by thousands of dollars worth of orthodontics. Albert looked inside. The only contents were peanut butter, canned soup and juice.

"So you'll know, I was also planning on taking a pot and a can opener and some bread."

"It's only food. All the stuff in this house and you only took food?"

"I can't eat diamonds. Well, I used to be able to but as of late they give me indigestion."

"Who are you?"

"I am a man of the world, if the world would have me."

"You make no sense. Where do you come from?"

"From my mother's womb. For being rich you aren't very wise, Old Man. May I go now? Can we put this incident behind us?"

Albert thought for a moment. He should want to press charges, but for what? Disrupting his sleep and stealing peanut butter? He would look petty and not very compassionate, which wouldn't go over well with his political friends with whom he needed to keep up appearances. Miriam's charity group would also scoff at such treatment.

"You might as well take some caviar to make it worth your while."

"No doing, Old Man, that rich stuff could kill me. Or perhaps that's what you're hoping for."

"Not in the least. You can go. But tell me who you are."

"No."

"Then I'll have you arrested."

"I don't believe you could catch me, but since you seem to like me, my name is Bert."

"Just Bert?"

"Are you trying to steal my identity? You thieves never give up, do you?" Bert grinned through his mocking tone of offense.

"A name."

"Bert Oldham."

"Take the food then and go. And take one of these damn copper pots with you as well."

"What was it?" Miriam asked groggily when he crawled back into bed. She'd already fallen back to sleep. Heaven forbid his safety interfere with her rest.

"Just the cat."

"I thought I heard talking."

"You must have been dreaming."

~ 2 ~

Albert couldn't get Oldham out of his head. It was ridiculous. At his desk he'd be signing whatever form wouldn't go through without his valuable signature and find himself pondering Oldham's comeback of being a man of the world if the world would have him. Didn't everyone feel that way now and then? The man was frighteningly ugly and Albert amused himself with the thought of starting a circus with Bert the Brute as a sideshow freak. The man's parts didn't fit together quite right as if he were made up of different bits like the world's ugliest Mr. Potato Head. No wonder the world didn't accept Bert Oldham. With his money, Albert had groomed himself into a handsome and debonair man. People in any room he entered were drawn to him as if the Pearl class and charm might wear off on them. Albert knew if Bert walked into a room, people would be afraid of catching the ugly and retreat to the opposite corner.

But yet his features didn't stop Bert from having and honing a sharp wit and quick tongue. Probably his looks forced these skills.

He needed to stop thinking of the man. It was unnatural. He'd even forgotten to call Sheila and she'd been livid. Good lord, one missed phone call and she became more of a harpy than Miriam.

Screw it. He had to know who Bert Oldham was.

"Nora," he buzzed his assistant, "can you look up that PI I used for the Jennings case?"

"Certainly, sir."

The investigator had no trouble finding Oldham. People quickly remember ugly men with sharp tongues.

"No home, no family to speak of. He showed up in Portland about eight months ago from what I've gathered."

"Where does he live if he doesn't have a house?"

The investigator gave Albert an *are-you-serious* look.

"Well, he must live somewhere."

"He's never reported to a shelter. He was rumored to have lived in Forest Park for some time, but as of late he spends most nights along the Springwater path just south of the Ross Island Bridge. There's a group of them and he's become the mayor of their little herd."

"Bring him to me."

~ 3 ~

"Mr. Pearl, there is a man here to see you." Nora said *man* as if she wanted to say "piece of crap I can't remove from my shoe." Albert pictured her nose wrinkling as she spoke.

"Is it Mr. Oldham?"

"He says he's afraid to give his name because it's all he's got. Shall I call security?"

Albert smiled to himself. This was exactly who he needed around.

"Absolutely not, send him in."

Bert, dressed in the same clothes Albert had seen him in the night of the robbery, entered Albert's office. Albert gave instructions to the PI to not tell Bert why he was being called in, just that it might interest him. When he walked in, Albert didn't miss the double take, but Bert recovered without pause.

"Ah, missing your peanut butter, are you? Don't worry, I might have some left. No one liked it much. That organic stuff tastes like dirt and even my people have some standards."

"Who are *your* people?"

"You know, people. Two legs, oversized brains. Mine have an enormous talent of piling their belongings into shopping carts. But between you and me, too many of them rot their brains with cheap booze."

"And you don't drink?"

"I didn't say that. I like wine, I'm just particular."

"You have a favorite wine?"

"Yes, whatever I can find in a rich man's house. I didn't get around to it, but I bet you have a superb wine cellar."

"So you have taste?"

"And sight, and smell. Although sometimes people are put off by the smell. And the sight, come to think of it."

Albert chuckled, "And your family?"

"Dead."

"Oh, I'm so sorry."

"Well, no, I mean I can only assume they're dead. When I left them they were all sleeping and looked dead so it's possible they *are* dead. You can't ever rule out possibilities. Which is why I'm here."

"Why are you here?"

"The possibility of curiosity. Luckily, I'm not a pussy. Cat, I mean. Otherwise, you know, the whole 'curiosity killing' thing would have wiped me out years ago."

Albert was beyond amused. He couldn't remember having a more intriguing conversation. He wondered when the last time was he could talk to someone without them deferring to him (the politicians he financed, the presidents of the companies he owned, his mistress when she wanted something) or him kowtowing to them (his wife, his tax advisor, and his mistress when she threatened to tell his wife).

No one spoke to him as a friend or equal, there was always an unspoken ranking of power he'd achieved an intuitive talent at. But Bert, now he was fun. This homely man with the fast tongue didn't care who Albert was or what he owned. He showed up to a stranger's office out of curiosity and hadn't missed a step yet.

"I'd like you to be my assistant."

"I don't work. If I worked I'd have to do taxes and have you seen those forms? Why doesn't the government take out the right amount in the first place is what I can't figure out."

"Then be my friend."

"This is how you get friends?" Albert shrugged. "Apparently you need some then. Alright then, what's your name?"

"Albert Pearl."

"Very well, Albert Pearl, Bert Oldham at your friendship."

~ 4 ~

And so the richest man in Portland became friends with one of the poorest. Wherever Albert went, Bert wasn't far behind, and sometimes ahead. He'd burst into a room announcing Albert's arrival, as everyone shrank from the man who became known as "Albert's toad."

Although Bert allowed Albert to buy him a few changes of clothes, he insisted they come from Target, not from Albert's personal tailor saying, "The clothes won't lay right on someone as awkward as me, so might as well go with the clothes that are already cut poorly to save the disappointment."

Albert was thrilled to have what his wife referred to as a "playmate." Miriam delighted in it at first. In her mind, it was better than him screwing his mistress. She knew Sheila ended the affair soon after Bert appeared on the scene. Albert never had quite gotten the hang of deleting the texts from his phone and the last one had read: "I can't compete w/ Bert. L8R." Since that message Albert hadn't been sneaking out of bed in the middle of the night to make phone calls (did he really think she didn't notice?) and played cards with Bert in the game room all night instead.

The delight didn't last.

After a couple months it grew embarrassing. The Toad tagged along everywhere with them. His silly comments, which amused her at the start, became an annoyance in short time. Bert was showing up with Albert at awards ceremonies, at political galas, at any of the myriad of events she and Albert attended to glad-hand and tighten connections. How was one to keep up the show of dignity and garner respect with a court jester in tow?

After another couple of months people began to talk. At tea with the governor's wife and other important ladies of the state, the question was asked if Albert still slept in the same bed as Miriam or had he set up bunk with Bert. Miriam joined in with their laughter, and only years of training kept her cheeks from flushing. As it was usually she who delivered them, she knew an insult when she heard one.

Since when had she and her husband become the butt of the joke?

Since Bert, of course.

He had to go.

"It's getting on to be winter, dear," she said to Albert one day when she discovered a rare moment alone with him.

"Brilliant Miriam, you've learned to use the calendar."

That was the other annoyance. Albert wanted to be Bert. Or so it seemed. He'd taken to wearing off the rack clothes, eating Skippy peanut butter on white bread, and attempting to make witty remarks. She didn't know which was the worst. The clothes were quite shameful to be sure, but Albert simply wasn't witty. He could come up with excellent roundabout speeches to bewilder the board into throwing more money into one of his ventures from which he would receive the most profit, but quick and cunning remarks weren't in his skill set.

"What I'm saying is that Bert can't live on the streets in the winter. And since he doesn't use the shelters we as humanitarians and taxpayers provide people like him, he is at risk of freezing. I know you care for him and I'd hate for you to have to lose him."

"What are you saying? You know he won't accept a house, he won't even stay in the shed."

"My point exactly. He needs to move on for the winter. You could offer to have someone drive him somewhere nicer. Just for the winter, of course."

"Thank you Miriam. You are very thoughtful. I'll have Carlton take him south."

~ 5 ~

Carlton, the Pearl's chauffer for twenty years, showed a passionate servitude toward Miriam. Had the man not been so overweight she might have thrown herself at someone so slavishly devoted to her. Still, she always let him think an affair with her was in the realm of possibilities. It kept him responsive to her whims and secretive about her requests – Albert still didn't know about the four hundred dollar weekly spa treatments Carlton took her to.

Miriam knew with one word from her, Carlton would see to it Bert didn't return from the trip. The morning Carlton was set to show Bert the beauty of the southern Oregon Coast where the winters were mild, Miriam went to speak with him. She worked up a good set of tears first.

"Ma'am, what is the problem?"

"Oh Carlton, The Toad--" she gasped a terrific sob.

"Ma'am, if he has harmed you--" He shook his fist and his jowly cheeks flared red.

"He tried to rape me. While Albert was in the shower. He came at me with a knife. But I ran. I locked myself in the guest bathroom until he went away."

"He should never even think of touching you."

"I know. I wish he were dead." She sobbed on cue and begged Carlton with her eyes.

"I can't do it here."

"No, of course not. Just so it's done."

"Gladly, ma'am."

"Thank you, Carlton," she stroked his cheek, feigning love but hiding revulsion at the sweat he'd worked up from only a few angry sentences.

~ 6 ~

Carlton seethed as Mr. Pearl insisted Bert sit in the back seat of the Rolls. A man such as The Toad shouldn't even be inside a car such as this. The men in Carlton's family had served the wealthy in some capacity since the 17th century. It was in their blood to show respect, but to also deserve respect. They, like the lead cook and head housekeeper, were more than mere servants; they were the upper crust within the workings of the house. They knew when to anticipate a person's needs before the person was even aware they needed something. It was natural to them to make it seem natural to the people they served to be waited on hand and foot. They saw to it the house ran as perfectly as possible.

The Toad did not fit into that perfection. One did not just walk off the streets and know how to belong in a family such as the Pearls. The Toad did not seem to recognize this obvious fact of life. The resentment Carlton festered for Bert began upon report of Bert sitting to the right of Mr. Pearl at a dinner party. To the right was reserved for only the most important. This toad of a man was lower than dirt and had no breeding.

And now this offense against Mrs. Pearl.

It was time for The Toad to be gone. Forever. Men like him polluted the world of the privileged.

But trapped in Carlton's breeding and training was the need to do things properly, to allow a fair fight. There would be no shooting in the back or trickery that would leave Carlton feeling as if he'd disrespected the propriety of his own class.

"Choose where you will die," Carlton said as he flicked the child locks.

"I'll die where I lie down and don't wake up again."

"Enough of your ridiculous words. You'll die today. Choose where or I will take you to the police for raping Mrs. Pearl."

"Rape her? You must be joking. I've no interest in her. You should have gotten the news by now that I've no taste for classy things. She'd give me more trouble than fish paté."

"Choose."

"You're serious?"

"Quite. Choose and die like a man, or else face a prison cell with men who will make you wish you were dead."

"Fine. To Forest Park then. It was the first place I stayed in Portland. I like it there. So much so I wouldn't mind decomposing into a clump of trillium."

Carlton drove to a parking area few people used. The immense park, larger than some towns, suited Carlton. The body would be easy to dispose of without the effort of transporting it elsewhere.

"Get out," Carlton released the safety locks. Looking in the mirror he detested the expression on The Toad's face. No fear, no pleading, nothing but the usual silly smirk that was forever plastered on his face as if The Toad were always in on a joke you wouldn't get. The Toad got out of the car and waited for Carlton to pull himself out.

"Gonna make it, Old Boy?" Bert asked. "So, I get to choose where I die. Is this some bizarre aspect of your moral code that tells you murder is fine as long as the murderee gets to feel they're in a nice place? Strange, but it's your show. Still, what if I choose to run, Old Boy? You couldn't catch me. You're sweating bullets just getting out of the car."

"You wouldn't run. You're enjoying this too much."

"You're right on that. It's not every day I get to die. Tends to be a one off kind of deal, not much different than losing one's virginity – bit scary, not sure what to expect, possibly messy, and once it's done you can't go back."

"Would you shut your mouth for once."

"One last thing. There *is* a difference between this and losing the old cherry."

"What?"

"Far less likelihood of one of us ending up pregnant." Bert tilted his head toward Carlton waiting for a laugh or even a giggle. "You really have no sense of humor, Old Boy. Sad that. So much for the jolly fat man. Well, let's go. There's a divine spot with a great view. I'd love to rot there."

Bert took Carlton up one ridge and down the next. If Carlton lodged any complaint, Bert swore the paths must have been altered since his time there or that the various trail names confused him.

"Spruce Trail, Maple Trail, Redwood Trail. This might be easier on both of us if I'd paid better attention in biology. You alright, Old Boy?"

The driver wheezed. It had taken everything for him not to show any weakness. The hills were torment on his legs, back and heart. He wanted to shoot The Toad after the third climb, but his father's voice rang in his head reciting the lack of dignity in a man who shot another in the back. But now? He felt as if bricks had been laid on his chest. His father had killed a man that way – piling the bricks until the man could no longer breathe. That had been another one who didn't know his place. He'd run off with the daughter of the house - an act akin to social rape.

People needed to know when to stay within their class or else pay the price. It was why Carlton hoped Mrs. Pearl would never offer herself to him – although he dreamed of it. It was obvious she wanted him, but he would be torn between knowing his proper place and a duty to obey what she demanded. Carlton was pulled from his conundrum by The Toad's voice. It sounded so far away. Had The Toad run? Again, the lower class proving their lack of class. Pain seared through his body and the world shot him full off brilliant unbearable brightness, then black.

~ 7 ~

Albert was laughing.

"But how did you save him? No offense, Bert, but I don't take you for someone who keeps up their CPR card."

"No indeed. I've kissed enough dummies in my life."

And Albert laughed harder. The entire day he'd been looking for Bert, calling for him like a little girl trying to find her cat.

"Give up, dear," Miriam had said. "He's obviously run away from home."

"I don't think he'd leave without saying anything. What if he's in trouble? I never really know where he goes when he isn't here."

"We can put up lost and found posters. Really, Albert, he's a grown man with a mind of his own. He drifts and you knew that when you took up with him. You can't own a stray."

Albert didn't see Miriam's smirk when the Rolls pull up. He did however hear her groan when Bert called from the entryway, "Did anyone order one obese man? He's a bit out of sorts, but will probably be raiding the pantry by evening."

"Everything alright, Miriam? You don't look well."

"Bit of gas. Better go see what your toad is on about."

"I wish you wouldn't call him that."

"It suits him."

When Albert went out, Bert had Carlton's arm around his shoulder and was walking him over to the bench in front of the house.

"Carlton? Bert, what's happened?"

"Carlton and I went out for a bit. Okay, truth be told, I do believe he wanted to kill me. Don't be angry with him. Someone obviously set him up for it; I don't think he'd have come up with the idea himself. No offense Old Boy, but you're all about doing what you're told, not thinking for yourself. You really should reconsider that approach to life. I mean, look where it's gotten you."

"Bert, what are you talking about? Carlton tried to kill you?"

"He was very polite and genteel about it. But when I wanted to die in this beautiful little spot, well I *may* have gotten lost a few times, and I *may* have taken the ways with the biggest hills, and I *may* have given him a heart attack."

By now several other servants had come to see what the fuss was about. Albert ordered the cook to get in and call an ambulance, then the head housekeeper to stay with Carlton while he and Bert went up to the study. By the time they got there, Albert was laughing so hard tears were dripping from his eyes.

"So without the CPR—"

"Well, it's not Red Cross approved, but I camped with a Chinese man once who taught me all kinds of strange things. Did you know duckbills are actually rather tasty? Of course, the ducks do look a bit silly afterward. Anyway, the Chinaman showed me different ways to influence the body by simply giving a squeeze. I thought I'd forgotten it all, but once I'd given Carlton the heart attack I certainly couldn't just let him die."

"But he was going to kill you."

"He hadn't drawn a weapon so there was still a chance he might have a change of heart. Which apparently he did."

"Unless someone told Carlton to change his mind he wouldn't."

"Does someone have to tell him when to crap as well? Never mind, don't answer. So, suddenly my brain kicks in and I remember that a pinch to the tip of the pinky will stop a heart attack. To be honest I thought the Chinaman was full of crap when he told me this, but it seems to work."

"I wonder who would have wanted you dead?"

Bert shrugged, "I don't know, but they should have had the decency to wait in line behind all the others who are queued up to kill me. Taking cuts is so rude. So what shall we do today?"

"I think you should move in here. It would be safer."

"Safer? Your driver just tried to kill me. The streets have proven to be safer than Casa Pearl."

"Okay, it would be better for me. I like having you around. You make my day fun. I just think with as much as you're here, you might as well occupy one of the ten bedrooms we don't use."

~ 8 ~

After some initial reluctance, Bert decided living in a posh house would be something he'd never experienced. "And life is all about the experiences, Albert."

Miriam was furious. "I won't have that mongrel in one of my beds."

"You're being unreasonable. He'll be no trouble. You won't even know he's here."

"I always know when he's here. His stupid cackle and ugly features pierce through the woodwork. And I know once I hear that annoying laugh that soon you'll be chortling right along with him."

"You used to like him."

"For the first week."

"Look, if you let him stay you can tell your charity group of the wonderful thing you are doing by letting a homeless man share your home. Think how good it will make you look."

That got her. If there was anything Miriam loved more than being rich, it was having people think how the money hadn't changed her, how kind she was, and how giving. She thought of herself as the Princess Diana of Portland – rich, but yet always thinking of and caring for others.

"Fine, he can stay. But only through the winter."

~ 9 ~

Bert found it odd to lie in such a soft bed in such a warm room. The first week he couldn't sleep without opening the windows and moving the pile of down blankets to the floor. The house stifled him as if the walls, regardless of the spaciousness, penned in his thoughts. Miriam was thankful for his morose behavior as it kept his cackle at bay and she hoped Albert would recognize what his offer had done to Bert and send The Toad back to whatever brackish water he spawned from.

But Albert didn't. He'd grown too used to having Bert around and Bert was what he wanted. Albert's rank in life meant he no longer took into account other people's feelings, only how the other people made him feel or what they could do for him.

Miriam's loathing of Bert hadn't subsided. Albert's promise of her looking like a saint to her charity group hadn't been realized. Turned out homeless people were so last year. These days the rage was cleft palate children. That bitch Cassandra King was hosting two of them who were in town to get surgery to repair the malformation. An ugly homeless man who was homeless by choice couldn't stand up to two dark-eyed orphans. When the women laughed at her, Miriam's interest in promoting the end of Bert's life was renewed.

~ 10 ~

"Try some lobster, Bert," Albert insisted one evening at dinner. "It's delicious."

Miriam considered giving the lobster, flown in that morning from Maine and selected by one of New England's top chefs for its sweet meat, to someone like

The Toad would be more of a waste than giving it to a dog who would just throw it up on the rug. No one of Bert's class could understand or appreciate the texture, the superiority, the perfection of the dish. He would be better off eating fake crabmeat.

"No thanks, Old Man. I've never understood the desire to eat anything that smells as bad as fish. Besides, that lobster could have nibbled on a human body and I can't add cannibal to my list of vices. Oh, and I'm terribly allergic. Minor detail."

"What happens if you eat it?" Albert asked.

"Nothing more severe than what happens to a person allergic to bee stings. Just a tad dose of anaphylactic shock." Bert took a bite of his peanut butter on white bread.

"Must be terribly frightening." Miriam oozed compassion.

"Lucky for me dead fish are easier to run from than angry bees."

And Albert choked on his own hunk of white bread with peanut butter as he laughed at Bert's comment. Miriam rolled her eyes in disgust with her husband, but at least now she had a plan even The Toad couldn't talk his way out of.

~ 11 ~

"Cook," Miriam addressed the man who had prepared or planned every meal for the Pearls for the past ten years, "do you know a way to feature fish in a simple meal so that the person wouldn't taste it?"

"Why wouldn't you want to taste the fish? It should be the center of the meal."

"The person doesn't like fish."

"So why make them eat it?"

"Well, you know, fish is so good for you with all the protein and omega things and I just think it would be healthy."

"I could create a patè of salmon and chestnuts."

"No, too apparent. It has to be undetectable."

"I have been wanting to try a sausage in which fish is added. The flavor of the pork will hide any fish taste."

"Perfect. Can you prepare it for tonight?"

"Of course."

~ 12 ~

Bert's eyes swelled as he saw the large bockwurst being put on his plate. He scooped a pile of sauerkraut alongside it and squirted it all down with a flood of yellow mustard. Miriam saw Cook grimace at his creation being drowned without being sampled first.

"This looks wonderful. Finally, some simple food I can recognize."

"Dig in," Albert said as he took a bite. "This is the best sausage I've ever tasted." Cook beamed, never tiring of a compliment to his work.

Bert took a bite of the sauerkraut as Miriam mentally urged him to stop wasting time with rotted cabbage and eat the meat. "Mmm...gotta warm up the palate for the big show."

Two more mouthfuls of the cabbage and then Bert sliced into the sausage. Just as he was about to put it to his mouth, he paused.

"What's in this?" he asked the cook. "I smell pork, but also something else."

Miriam looked to Cook. He knew well enough how to answer.

"Some spices I wanted to try and a small amount of beef to round out the flavor."

"So you really made this yourself?"

"Bert, if you want to discuss things with Cook you do so after the meal. Not during. Now honor the man's work and eat."

"Sorry, my class is showing again."

And the bite of sausage went into his mouth. It was indeed the best sausage he'd ever tasted. As he began to slice another piece, his throat squeezed. He breathed in, but air wouldn't pass through to his lungs.

"Bert, everything okay?"

Bert shook his head. It felt like his eyes would pop.

"Are you choking?" Miriam faked concern. She got in position as if she would perform the Heimlich maneuver although she'd really rather not to have to touch The Toad.

Bert shook his head, then nodded his head. His face burned red. Albert slapped him on the back. "What do you need us to do?"

Bert gaped open his mouth like a fish out of water. Albert saw Bert's tongue was blue, then Bert collapsed. Albert did the only thing he could think of.

"Why are you pinching his pinky?" Miriam asked.

Albert, now in tears, sobbed, "I don't know what else to do."

~ 13 ~

Bert, much to Miriam's irritation, was buried in the Pearl family plot. She hated that even in death The Toad didn't know his place. Albert would take up with another mistress soon enough to entertain himself, but that was gossip every wife of her circle had spread about themselves. At least tolerating an affair was part of the territory of being a rich man's wife. Putting up with a husband mingling with the poor (unless it was as part of a charity that benefited one's reputation) was not. Albert needed to remember who he was.

Miriam saw to it he did.

Family Secrets

"Family Secrets" started with just the opening line. I brainstormed about why someone wouldn't want to open a door and settled on the obvious – to protect themselves from what might be out there. Unfortunately, the magazine that ran the contest, Writer's Journal, *went under just as I was ready to pack this one into the envelope.*

"Whatever you do don't open the door, okay, buddy?"

"Yeah, Dad." Caleb gave an exasperated sigh. They told him this every time they went out for their monthly date. Next would come mom and the curtains.

"And keep the curtains shut. Remember?"

"I know, Mom." As his mom's eyes pulled into a scolded puppy droop, Caleb felt bad for being snippy. He smiled at her. "I'll be careful. Now you two kids don't stay out too late."

"Good man." His father gave him a sturdy clap on the shoulder. Caleb could see the hair on his father's forearm sticking out of the cuff. He'd never really thought of his dad as a hairy guy, but he knew sometimes when people got older they got hairier. Look at the tufts coming out of Grandpa's ears and those gnarly rogue hairs poking from Gran-Gran's chin. And, he thought with pride, the hairs that sprouted above his own—

"My sweetheart." In the middle of thinking about his crotch, his mom interrupted with a kiss to his forehead. "There's fried chicken in the fridge. Oh, and don't eat too much junk food, especially chocolate."

"C'mon, Margie. Leave the boy be. I'm starving already and it's going to take us an hour to get there."

With another goodbye from his mom, Caleb closed the door behind them. He waited by the front window until he heard the car back out of the driveway. He didn't know or care where they went, but he did know and did care that they would be gone until at least midnight, one a.m. more likely. He thought it was silly he always had to stay home when they went on this date night thing they'd concocted. Any other night he was allowed to go to his friend Aaron's house, but on date night his parents insisted he stay home, lock the doors, and keep the curtains shut tight. He could only figure they had some paranoia about the house being robbed, but no concern about the burglar stealing their only child.

Old people made no sense.

But it didn't matter that he couldn't go out. This date night he was prepared. He'd waited up all last night to download Dogs of Vengeance III when it first went live and had resisted playing it all day. His mom hated violent video games – odd given her no-qualms attitude about slaughtering their backyard chickens – and he really wanted to play this game on the 60-inch plasma in the front room. Plus, he had a hidden stash of peanut M

& M's he planned to devour while he played. The candies usually made him nauseous if he ate too many, but he'd limit himself to one bag.

As soon as the Prius shifted from reverse to drive and hummed away, Caleb ran to get his laptop. Aaron had been texting him all day to come over and play the new game, but Caleb wanted to play alone first, to savor his $60 purchase in world-crushing, alien-blasting solitude. He set the TV to receive the wireless signal from the computer and pulled the controller from his back pocket. Time to create his avatar.

Just as he'd finished making himself into a 6 foot 4 German stormtrooper, his phone rang. Caleb sighed and threw down the controller to pull the phone out of his other back pocket. He looked at the caller ID before answering.

"Hey, Aaron."

"Dude, you play it yet?"

"I was trying to." He cradled the phone between his cheek and shoulder, picked up the controller and selected his first weapon.

"Oh my god, dude, how could not have played it yet?"

"Dude, I told you I was waiting to play it on the 60-inch."

"Oh, hell yeah. Look, trust me, it sucks with only one player. I'm coming over."

"Dude, you can't. My parents'll rip me a new one."

"C'mon, we'll just clear the first two levels and I'll go. They'll never know."

"I dunno."

"Dude, don't be a pussy."

"I'm not a pussy, man, it's just—"

Aaron interrupted with a convincing *meow*.

"Fine, but you are outta here by 11:00."

"Yeah, yeah. See ya in ten."

Caleb tossed his phone aside, shook his head over his idiot friend and continued to explore the game options. He began Level Zero that taught how to explore the Vengeance World, switch weapons and perform basic maneuvers. By the time he'd mastered jumps, shooting and swapping a laser gun for a radioactive sword he heard the clang of Aaron locking his bike to the handrail of the front steps. Caleb jumped off the couch and whipped the door open before Aaron could knock.

"You could wake the dead with that racket."

Aaron meowed at Caleb again as he walked in the house. He stopped once he saw the game paused on the big screen.

"Oh man, this is tight!"

They plunked down on the couch and battled their way through taking over the world. Level Two came and went. The teens ignored the clock as territories fell into their hands while they combatted aliens, borgs and Nazis and amassed an arsenal of weapons and treasure.

"I gotta take a mean piss," Caleb said as he paused the game on the stats page between Levels Four and Five. The pause mode brought up the TV clock.

11:57 flashed in bold blue letters against a grey background.

"Crap, dude, you gotta go."

Aaron didn't argue or make any cat noises. He knew it was time to go, not out of concern for his friend, but simply because Mr. and Mrs. Kaynus gave him the creeps. They were nice enough and all, but there was just something about them that sent his neck hairs on high alert.

Caleb followed Aaron out the door wanting to be on the lookout for any parental sightings. The last thing he remembered was how perfectly round the moon was that night.

~ ~ ~

"Caleb, Caleb. Get up," his father's voice urged him from somewhere far away. He tried to sit up, but his body ached and his stomach bulged worse than after Thanksgiving dinner. He plopped back down to the floor.

"Can't."

"Up now, mister."

His father pulled him upright and forced him to a standing position. Caleb opened his eyes and a girlish scream escaped his mouth. Aaron, well, parts of Aaron lay where Caleb had just been. The torso was missing most of its belly and an arm lay a few feet away from where it should be. Caleb thought he should want to puke, that puking would be the normal response. Instead, his stomach rumbled in hunger despite the feeling of being over filled already.

"We shouldn't have kept it from him." His mother wrung her hands.

"Kept what? What's going on?" Caleb looked down at his shirt. It was covered in blood. "Was I attacked?"

"You tell him. Margie. I've got to move that bike. What were thinking, Caleb?"

"Now, Dan, it's not his fault. You remember your first time. We should have told him sooner. We should have been there for him."

For the first time ever, Caleb yelled at his parents.

"What is going on? What are you talking about? Why aren't you calling the cops? Some psycho killed Aaron, could have killed me and you're bickering about me opening the door?"

"Not a psycho, dear," his mother said sweetly. "You."

"Me what?"

His father rolled in the bike. The broken lock dangled from the handlebars. Before he could ask how the lock broke, his father cut him off.

"We're werewolves, Caleb. You just ate your best friend. Where do you think your mother and I go every full moon?"

Caleb's head reeled.

"We wanted to keep it from you." His mother put her arm around him. The shock running through him left Caleb too numb to shrug her off. "We wanted to keep you our little boy, but we knew this day had to come. It would have been better if we'd been there for you."

"This is a joke, right? Some YouTube stunt?" He looked around the living room for a camera.

"We need to clean this up. Can you eat anymore, Dan?"

"You know I don't really like leftovers."

"I know, but I only had one hipster and they're never very filling. Wouldn't it be nice to eat together as a family?"

Caleb wanted to shake his mom and say enough was enough, but with the talk of leftovers and the hipster and the smell of Aaron's blood filling the room he couldn't ignore the hunger welling up inside him. He wanted to eat some—

Before he could finish the thought, his mom flung open the living room curtain. She was doused in moonlight. Within seconds, she dropped to the floor, sprouted lush grey fur and an elegant muzzle. On long legs, she trotted over to Aaron and began gnawing his thigh. Her tail wagged as she crunched through the femur.

"C'mon, son. Time to learn responsibility. You always clean up after yourself. That's the first lesson. We'll teach you more after this is done."

Caleb's dad took his son's hand as if he was a little kid who might get lost. They stepped into the moonlight. A jolt of pain jagged through his body as it shifted into its new shape. This time he was aware of what was happening. The delicious scent of blood and flesh teased his senses sending his stomach rumbling. He strode over to Aaron with his dad following behind. The three feasted their way through the tender teenage flesh and crunched into marrow-filled bones. When nothing was left, Caleb whined. It had been the best meal he'd ever tasted.

Part Four

MIDNIGHT

Island Ways

Unlike my ocean-loving-bordering-on-ocean-obsessive husband, I have serious qualms about swimming in a giant body of water that has things such as sneaker waves, strong currents and riptides. This story reflects my take on (and perhaps validation of) those fears. "Island Ways" won Honorable Mention in the Writer's Journal Horror Writing Competition and was published in their magazine.

With a harsh jolt, I landed in the sand and a scrawny brown man stood over me clucking away as if spitting venom with sounds. A boy in crimson shorts plopped down next to my head.

"He say, 'Crazy white fool, she not ready for you yet.'"

Then the old man spat on the ground so close to my ear I heard it *thunk* into the sand. He stepped over me and continued on with whatever he'd been up to before dashing me to the ground.

I flicked my eyes to the boy who grinned at my glance and then readjusted to rest on my elbows.

"What was that about?" The tide rippled rhythmically and I longed to get in to wash the sand off.

"You almost touch the water," the boy chirped.

Of course I did. With palm trees, thatched huts, blinding sand and a warm turquoise expanse calling for me to dive in, this remote South Pacific island was a living postcard. My magazine had assigned me an enviable task: report on the island culture and photograph the scenery as part of a compare-contrast feature of "undiscovered" locales. After eighteen hours of flights and being motored over by a crew who refused to speak to me or look me in the eye, I was dying to rinse the travel grunge off in this paradisiac sea that whispered my name.

But the instant I stepped forward, my toes only centimeters from the sea, that old codger threw me down with more force than I could have believed possible from such a little fellow. From the glare beneath his furrowed brow and harsh string of syllables, he was obviously not happy about me being here. I thought perhaps he didn't want his home's beauty splashed across six pages of glossy urging other "crazy white fools" to come with their condo developments and Micky Ds.

So, I was confused by the boy's answer that the man's anger stemmed, not from my existence, but from me almost touching the water. I expected something like "my grandfather thinks you're a right bastard," but the comment of this puppy-like boy who'd followed me since I unpacked in his father's guest hut (which was surprisingly luxurious) made no sense.

"What do you mean? I want to go for a swim."

The boy stared at me as if I'd just asked to have sex with his goat.

"No, you no swim here. Up to river is where swim is safe."

I looked to the glass-like water, then back to him. Before leaving home I'd read about this area and, for the tropics, it sounded risk-free – sea snakes were unheard of, sharks didn't like the shallow, and only the roughest storm caused any wave action. "Perfectly safe here." I stood to wade into the water that swelled with invitation.

The boy seized my ankle.

"Sir, no," he pleaded. Tears rimmed his eyes. "I show you good place."

Worrying his father might arrive and wonder what I'd done to make his child cry, I gave in. We trudged through the jungle to a lovely swimming hole. It wasn't the warm, buoyant South Pacific I longed for – even paddling behind the waterfall I wanted to leave the boy and run back to the sea's aquamarine embrace – but I felt refreshed.

"We having big banquet for you tonight," he said between splashes.

"Really, why?"

"To show you island ways."

Ah yes, the dog and pony show all small island chiefs felt compelled to put on. The festivities stretched the food supply, inconvenienced the women who made all the preparations, and were completely unlike the daily life of the island. But the chiefs liked to show off.

Evening approached and the bustle made me feel I should be helping. Instead, I was repeatedly told to sit. Finally, I did, making notes of the activity and weaseling over to question the women about what they were cooking as the boy translated. Long lists of fruits and birds in spicy sauces rambled out of him as he tried to keep up with the cooks' menu.

"Why no fish?" I asked.

The boy again shot me the you-offend-my-goat look. I waited for his translation. Why wouldn't island people eat fish? It didn't get any simpler than stepping in and jabbing or grabbing something to grill up.

"We only eat fish that wash up on beach."

"But you have a whole fish market only steps away. You just swim out and get some. I could show you." I wanted to show him. Despite my hunger and exhaustion, I yearned to dive into that sea and swim away. The child appraised me with his eyes looking for the possibility of my insanity.

His father approached us alongside an attractive woman dressed in a flowery sarong and hair decorated with shells and ribbons. I thought she might be his wife, but the child, seeing his opportunity for escape, ran off calling for his "mama." I stood feeling awkward as I towered over the two.

"Mister, this is Atiri. She would like to be with you before the festivities."

A whore? This lovely thing was passed around to visitors my host wanted to impress? I shook my head, "No offense, but I'm married."

Atiri giggled, "I only want to talk to you. We'll sit in public view if you're worried you can't resist me."

At her phrase "can't resist" my thoughts flew not to her, not to my wife, but to the ocean whose waves taunted me as each ripple licked the sand.

"Sorry, my mistake." I gestured and we sat down. "You want to talk to me?"

She looked to my host. He nodded back, and then clasped my shoulder, "Listen to her, we are not naïve islanders. What she says is true." He stroked Atiri's hair and walked away.

Atiri began her tale.

"I don't know when my people arrived here or how long we spent at sea, but once we came we loved this land. Too long in boats, many think instills a love of the sea, but we wanted land. Once we got here, we stayed. Unfortunately, the ocean wanted us back after having us for so long. She saw us as hers and became jealous of our love for our island. She hated seeing us feeding ourselves on something other than her gifts as we gathered fruit and ate the land's small animals. She thought—"

"The sea thought?"

Atiri scolded me with her eyes. I tried to still my judgment.

"The sea thought she was the only one for us, that we had turned our backs on her. When we tried to go back in, to fish or play, she became angry and conjured up terrible storms. We cursed her and this angered her further. It came to the point where she refused to forgive us. The moment one of us stepped in, she formed into a monster to devour us. Any guests we gave host to were treated as one of us and also taken by her. She hates us, but still taunts us by not letting us abandon our desire for her. All men are drawn to the sea, but we on this island feel it tenfold."

I smiled at the fable, but held my tongue. She seemed intelligent, how could she believe these tales? We sat together through the meal with my host on my opposite side smiling at my companionship with Atiri. As the sun began to crawl down the sky toward the ocean's line, I again fought the urge to go for a swim and thought of Atiri's story. Could the sea really beckon people in? I smirked at my own thought, picturing the ocean as an old barfly trying to sweet talk the barkeep for "just one more" vodka martini. My grin didn't go unnoticed.

"You are happy with this evening?" Atiri asked.

"Quite," I suppressed my giggle.

"Good," said my host, "now we show you the essence of our island."

I expected a native dance I would politely applaud. Instead, Atiri stood up and dropped her clothes. Any sarcasm within me lost itself at the sight of her.

"Follow me."

I did. Her voice urged me just as the ocean had done all day. I couldn't resist. I thought of the head bashing my wife would give me before realizing my host and several others were following. I breathed a sigh of relief – and perhaps a little frustration.

We paused on the beach although I wanted to continue running toward the water. I stopped at the sight of my elderly assailant glaring at me while muttering. It seemed the waves grew louder, but I put it off as an illusion created by the old man's rhythmic incantations. Then I looked at the sea. The water that barely rippled this afternoon now churned into foam as it bit into the beach. Instinctively, I stepped back.

Atiri stepped in front of the old man. He continued chanting as the waves gained volume and size. It sounded like a heavy storm approaching, but no wind stirred the trees and the sky remained clear.

The sun met the horizon as Atiri stepped toward the jet engine noise of furious waves.

"Atiri, no." I ran forward, but someone grabbed me.

"This is our island," my host hissed into my ear. "This is our way. You believe now, don't you?"

Atiri glanced back at me and pointed. White water washed over her feet. That's all it took. The sea had gotten a taste and wanted more. In a scene my nightmares couldn't create, the water shaped itself into a creature more tooth and claw than body. In a cat-like motion it sprang at Atiri and yanked her from us. The sea calmed itself before the horizon swallowed the sun. Blood washed onto the shore as I stared in disbelief. My host loosened his grip.

"This is the truth of our island. We are not a place for travelers."

"Just visitors though. Atiri," my throat tightened, "said the ocean only hated your people."

"Visitors are seen as our guests, as one of us. White men have come, it is how we learned English, but few can resist the Demon's call. We do not want more to die for the ocean's jealousy. We appease her on occasion, much like your spousal support in a divorce. And she tolerates us, but will never let us forget the wrongs she thinks we did her."

"You kill your own people," I accused.

"One sacrifice a year, but for that year the chosen person lives as a god in luxury. The ocean is tricked into thinking we are losing our best. This makes her happy. Still, she will take anyone who steps in. And we want to go in; we feel the pull just as you have. We hope one day she will forget her feud, but until then this island will never be more than it is."

The old man approached us and dragged his index finger in the space between my eyebrows. Whatever he'd smeared on crinkled my skin underneath as it dried. He clucked his sounds at me. The boy, again by my side, interpreted:

"He say, 'Your year begins.'" He turned to his father, "We go back to the Next One's party now?"

A rush of confusion was replaced with realization. I was too shocked to scream, painfully aware I'd been trapped by Atiri's pointing finger. My entire body pulsated with the need to escape.

My host cowered me with a look that told me not to try anything. I wanted to run, but to where? This tiny island and its carnivorous sea served better than any prison bars or city walls. I shook with the knowledge of my impending death until my eyes found the old man shooting me a snide brown-toothed grin.

It steadied me.

I would live my year as a god and, as I waded in to meet my doom, I knew to whom my finger would point.

Purge

What happens when I find a quarter on the ground? Elation at my luck? No, my mind unravels a myriad of paranoid possibilities, "Purge" is one of them. I had fun with the different personalities arguing around the table – anyone who's attended a meeting at work will relate to them.

"Excuse me sir, could you spare a quarter?"

Polite laughter rose and fell as Rhett moved aside a Plexiglas box big enough to hold a cat, but containing only a quarter.

"That's exactly the point, Nick," Rhett continued. "No one bothers picking up dimes anymore and pennies are tossed aside everyday. But a quarter laying on the sidewalk will be snatched up instantly."

"How many sites we talkin' about?" asked Hank.

"We've gone over this, Tex," Nick huffed.

"Maybe I missed a meetin' or two since *I'm* workin' on somethin', not sittin' on my duff."

"I'm not just sitting around. Programming is my assignment - an assignment that *I've* completed."

"What're you implying?" Tim asked.

"Just that *some* people finish their work while others seem to struggle."

"We all have a task to do, Nick. I think we're right on target," Rhett said. He regretted bringing Nick on the team. The guy never worked well with others, but with a few lines of programming he had obtained a key resource for the cause – thousands of quarters. Still, he wished Nick would stop goading anyone who took the bait. "Tim, please brief us on your progress."

"Hank and I finished the formula. We've dubbed it Purge. Released airborne one part per billion wiped out fifty rats in a room larger than this. But airborne Purge kills at random, so we formulated a coating activated by oils on the victim's fingers. We took time developing the formula properly to target only humans."

"Yeah, Nick," Hank said, "remember we're doin' this to cull humans off this planet so other species can have a chance. You want us to rush around and take out everything? Some of us have bigger worries than a few lines of code and which Coke machine to hit next."

"Okay guys. Enough," Rhett ordered. "Stan, you've planned the targets?"

Stan went to the podium.

"Well," he said peering over his glasses, "we could go big – hit excess-filled L.A. or wasteland New York. But that's so Al-Qaeda - all show, no substance."

"So what's your suggestion? I thought we were making a statement," Nick criticized.

"Nick, can it," Rhett said.

"We don't want to raise alarms," Stan continued. "If we release these quarters in a big city the media will be alerted within an hour. No, we start in small places - towns, rural areas, little suburbs that have encroached on natural spaces. If we get those places back for Mother Nature, she'll begin to rebound. I've compiled a list." He handed a sheet around and the same list appeared on the screen behind him. "Rhett, can you fly over all these within a week? That's the optimal time frame. Then we'll do a second wave of mid-sized cities."

Rhett scanned the paper. The Cessna could handle the flights, but with the weight of the quarters and an assistant--

"I'll need to refuel often."

"It'll be fine," Stan pushed up his glasses, "regional cooperatives will refuel you. I'll get you their info."

"Sounds like you've got *your* end under control," Nick eyed Tim and Hank, the project's chemists.

"Shut it, Dweeb. You know we've had the hardest component," Tim said. "Until Rhett takes flight, Hank and I are the only ones putting ourselves at risk every day. You think working with something more deadly than Serin is fun?"

"*You* volunteered for it," Nick said. "*You* responded to the ad just like the rest of us."

"Oh, I feel so bad for you. You must be developing a nasty case of carpal tunnel after all that typing. Wearing a wrist support, that's right up there with daily exposure to neurotoxins."

"I'm just saying, you made the choice."

"And I'm choosing to risk my life for the planet. I'm willing to be exposed to this to knock humans down a few notches and let Nature gain an even playing field. You've only risked eyestrain."

"Now," Rhett said before Nick made his comeback, "Stan will provide a run down of his plan. Then Tim and Hank can demo their work." Without looking Rhett sensed Nick shifting in his seat waiting to be recognized. "And afterward Nick can take us down the hall to demonstrate his skills against the vending machine."

Stan tapped on the computer. A U.S. map with red dots scattered from coast to coast appeared on the room's screen.

"If we hit the areas I've designated, we should take the population down by a third within a week. That's good, but for humans to return to a population the planet can support through hunting and gathering and sustainable agriculture we need to get it down by seventy percent. This will occur in the second wave on mid-sized cities I mentioned." Blue dots scattered the map alongside the red dots. "In addition, operatives in other countries will take Purge and place it on their coins. We're coordinated to begin in one month. Humans have made a mess of Earth and we need to clean it up. Within six weeks the newly purged planet will begin renewing itself. Tim, Hank, could you explain what you've developed?"

An image of a quarter replaced the map.

"There's your ordinary quarter," Hank drawled. "Anyone seein' it layin' on the street, in a field, hell even in a cow pie, ain't gonna hesitate to pick it up--"

"That was my research," Nick interrupted. "I put out coins and the quarters were always picked up. I did the monitoring and data collection."

"Please, Nick," Rhett said, "we'll get to your part."

"As Nick brilliantly discovered, people like quarters," Hank continued. "Tim and I worked with various neurotoxins from venoms to botulinum. We formulated one that's stable in spore form."

"Please explain that," Rhett asked.

"Spores can sit around forever with all the fixin's necessary to do their job, but just waitin' for the right conditions. Our conditions are quite specific so we don't wipe out all the other critters. We conjured up somethin' that's activated only by oil on a human hand--"

"How the hell do you do that, Tex?"

"It doesn't matter for this discussion, Nick," Rhett seethed. "What was your estimated final population, Stan?"

"Conservative models show one billion, very likely less."

"And there's no risk of harming other species?"

"No," Tim answered, "the oils on the human hand are very specific. Purge reacts instantly with the oil and absorbs into the body. Death by system shutdown occurs within two minutes. The brain basically stops and the body up and quits." A cartoon hand grabbed the quarter. Tiny skulls and crossbones swam from the coin into the hand. An image of a gravestone with R.I.P carved on it morphed onto the screen. "Also, Purge biodegrades back into its component molecules. After a week the quarters become harmless coins again."

Nick snorted.

"Problem?"

"You chemists always think you know what you're doing, but end up creating things like Round-up and making things worse."

"We've analyzed this to pieces. We know what we're doin'."

"That's what they all say."

"A demonstration?" Rhett interrupted.

Tim took Stan's place at the podium and removed the Plexiglas box's lid. From under the podium he brought out a white rat. It sniffed the air as Tim stroked it several times before placing it in with the quarter and quickly snapping on the lid.

"You said only human oil would work," Nick sneered. "That's a rat in case you didn't notice."

"In case *you* didn't notice," Hank answered, "he pet the rat first."

"Oh, like that's enough?"

"Why don't you stick your greasy face in there and find out?" Tim snapped.

"I'm sick of this crap from you two," Nick launched out of his seat and punched Tim staggering the chemist back a few steps.

Only Rhett and Stan noticed the rat collapse. Its chest heaved twice, then nothing.

"Guys," Rhett shouted, "careful."

"Yeah idiot, the toxin's activated *in case you didn't notice.*" Tim grabbed the box forcing Nick to look. As Tim jutted the chamber toward him, Nick delivered a second punch. Instead of Tim's face, Nick's fist met the chamber, knocking it from Tim's hands. The rat and the quarter rolled onto the table.

~ ~ ~

The cleaning lady ignored the room that evening. The "In Use" sign was still lit and she'd been yelled at more than once for disturbing meetings when she only wanted to collect the bin bags. After a week of seeing the illuminated "In Use," she sighed and knocked on the door knowing none of these people bothered to empty their own trash. Plus, by now the carpet would be in sore need of a vacuum.

When there was no response to her knock, she opened the door. The stench forced her to drop the key as her hand flew to cover her nose and mouth. She didn't scream. After years of hospital janitorial work, the sight of dead bodies didn't faze her. While holding her breath she crossed herself, mentally recited a Hail Mary, and pocketed the quarter on the table before calling security.

The Text

I'm still undecided whether I like "The Text" or not. It's another opening line inspired story and I had fun with tormenting the protagonist. It has its good points and bad points, but overall I think it's a fun (if that word can be used for such a dark tale) piece if you don't think too hard or try to "over read" the story. If you like it, thanks. If you hate it, well, at least it's short.

Not wanting to be one of "those" people yakking in the middle of the aisle, I set my phone to silent mode before entering the store. As I roam through the produce department shaking my head over Keith's favorite wisecrack about old people never buying green bananas, my thigh tingles as the phone wiggles its signal. I pull it out and check the caller ID out of habit. Keith. Ironic, but he can wait. I stick the phone back in my pocket and a few seconds later, it buzzes twice to indicate a message.

Once in my car, I flick open the phone and thumb through the menus to get to the text message.

"Body disposed. Meet @ Lotus 10pm. Paymt due ASAP."

Very funny, Keith. Payment due. I owe him $10 for our weekly bet regarding which office female Gerald, our boss, would get rejected by this week. I guessed Sheila, his desperate secretary, but Keith gambled on the horse-faced new girl, Molly. Gerald took his chances on the new girl, got turned down in a heartbeat and Keith won the bet.

I hadn't been to the Lotus in months and couldn't believe Keith even knew where it was. He was a fun guy to talk to and joke with at work, but I never really thought of hanging out with him outside of work. Keith was, well, to put it bluntly, a complete nerd – thick glasses, starched checked shirt buttoned up to his chin, and white socks for every occasion. The running joke, which he went along with, centered on how even with his Sicilian roots, the mob would reject someone as dorky as him.

At 9:30 p.m., I shave and dress, at least hanging out next to Keith will make me the attractive one of the duo. I still can't believe the guy knows where the Lotus is; he doesn't even know the name of the bar closest to his apartment. Maybe he thinks the Lotus is a Thai restaurant. I walk the few blocks from my loft to meet up with Keith who I'm sure will be looking a bit silly trying to order Pad Thai from the bartender.

Inside the Lotus, the brick red walls absorb most of the light. Still, I scan the room for Keith and for any ex-girlfriends who might be lurking in my old haunting ground. I figure Keith'll stick out like a thumb on a cat, but I can't find him. I order a beer and glance around again. Maybe this is Keith's idea of a joke, not the body part, but tricking me into going out on Sunday, the deadest night of the week.

Finally, I spot him. He's sitting in a corner booth sipping a martini looking like he owns the place. His too thick glasses still perch on his face, but the black silk button down and tousled hair make him look like any other hipster who might loiter at the club.

I slide into the booth and he chokes on his olive.

"What're you doing here?" His eyes dart around the room.

"Got your text."

He doesn't even glance at me - his eyes are too busy peering into every corner of the room. "What text?"

"Meet you here at ten, payment due." Keith mutters something while shushing me like a school marm as I slap down two fives and say, "And what's with the body disposal? Your brother finally leave town?"

"Shut up," Keith blurts as two men stop in front of our table. One is big, football player big, while the other looks like a living Armani ad.

"You conducting other business, Keith? Should we step aside?" the big one asks in a condescending tone.

"Or is he in on this too?" Armani accuses, "You said one third, Keith. I ain't taking less than a third."

"Shut up you nitwit, I'll take care of everything. Did you find Marcus like I asked?"

"He's coming right now," the big one says and from behind him I can see another man in all black coming toward us. He looks like a character from a gangster movie set in the twenties and would have fit in perfectly a few years ago when the swing craze raged anew.

Keith, who earlier gave the impression of being calm and in charge, begins to fidget with his swizzle stick in the same way he does with his pen whenever Gerald wants him to present a report at a meeting. The confusion over the situation and Keith's attitude is more than I can handle. I grab my beer and try to stand up, "Look, sorry I interrupted. I'll catch you tomorrow."

Keith, using more strength than I would have guessed his scrawny frame possessed, pushes me back down. "Sit and keep your mouth shut. I'll take care of this." The other two slide in. I'm trapped.

"Take care of what?" I demand.

"Shut up," he seethes. The man in black stops at the table.

"Why're there four of you? Is this a trick, Keith?"

"No, Marcus," Keith says, "just a misunderstanding."

"Look, if I could just go," I say. "I thought this table was free—"

The man hammers his fist down on the table close enough to my beer to make it tilt and slosh over the edge. Keith cups his hand over the top to steady it. I want to guzzle the pint and get the hell back home. The noise of the bar's tinny stereo system is enough to drown out the sound of the fist, but no one could miss the body language of a bear about ready to strike out. The man notices a handful of regulars watching, straightens up and laughs. "Free, that's a good one."

As people go back to their flirting and drinking, he hovers back over the table.

"So Keith, we have two problems. You've let someone else in on this who wasn't supposed to know. This makes me wonder if you're a cop, only a cop would do something so stupid as to bring another person in at the end of a deal."

Keith bristles. "It's already taken care of, Marcus, just like your other problem."

"Yeah?" The guy beams a smile at Keith and he would have looked genuinely likeable if I didn't have a deep instinctive urge to run as far from him as possible. "You're good at solving my problems. Probably the best. But no money changes hands until this," he jerks his head in my direction, "is out of my sight."

"It's not a problem," Keith's voice remains flat.

Marcus laughs again. "Exactly." He turns to leave. "I'll be at my table when you're free."

The two others move out of the booth, but I just sit there. What is Keith? The text was a joke, right?

"Drink your beer and let's get you out of here," he commands. I chug the pint and then scramble out of the high-backed booth that looms over as if threatening to swallow me alive. Keith ushers me outside. The other two men follow.

"What's going on?" I notice my words are slurred. That usually takes a lot more than one beer, but I did drink it pretty fast.

"Just come on," Keith tugs on me and walks me into the park across from the Lotus.

"You're in big trouble from the boss," Armani says.

"Boss?" My head swims. All those Sicilian jokes – was there a reason Keith never denied them, just played along? "The text wasn't a joke, was it?" All my sibilant words slosh into themselves.

"You texted him?" the big one asks. "You knew this was supposed to be kept quiet."

"Yeah murder usually is," Keith snaps back.

Murder? My legs weaken under me. "I think I need to get home."

"You're not going home. Just take a seat here. You know you should really mind your drink in a place like that." I can't argue with him or fight my way back to standing as he guides me onto a secluded bench.

"Why? What are you, dude?"

"I kill people for money," he replies as if saying he collected stamps.

"No, you program the--" My mind fuzzes and I fight for the word, "typing boxes."

"Computers," Keith offers. "I never could give up my day job, keeps the tax man off my back, Sorry about the text, must have misdialed. Tough break, man, but business is business."

My eyes begin to close and an image flashes of his hand cupped over my beer.

"Did you--? Why? I wouldn't have told," I can barely understand my own words. My tongue feels like a stone in my mouth.

"Marcus would have tracked you down and killed you anyway. His methods aren't quick. This way is better. When people at work get the news that you died of a heroin overdose, I'll be sure to say it must be a mistake. Don't worry, man, I'll stand up for you."

I hear them walking away - the click of six dress shoes on pavement. I try to call them back.

I can't make my mouth work, saliva drizzles out, and my limbs rattle from a seizure. Then for a moment I'm calm and the street light above me fades to black.

Transcription of Taxi 6473

The idea of this story – another Myths Gone Modern tale – was in my head for a few months, building and adding to itself, but never really coalescing into a plot line that would pull it together. It finally got its life kicked into it and put onto paper when a first line contest called for the opening line to be "This conversation is over..." I instantly saw a police sergeant arguing with an underling who'd transcribed something disturbing. It ended up being one of my favorite stories.

"This conversation is over, Anderson."

"Sergeant, I really think we need to look into this."

The sounds, the screams still echoed in my head.

"Anderson," The Sarge glared at me across the desk with his dark eyes - the eyes I knew the front desk girls dreamed about. All I dreamed of lately was the shrieking and the wet slash of skin and muscle being sliced open. "Never bring this up again. Got it?"

"But sir, this is big. We need to go to the—"

"Go to the what? Who do you go to with this? Look," his voice lowered to a soothing tone, but I still sensed the irritation behind it, "what you heard, what you *think* you heard on that tape is nothing. A murder. One of many the NYPD are unlikely to solve."

"But the matter is being classified as a suicide, sir."

"Well, there you have it," he threw up his hands. "No other explanation for it."

"Sir," I shook my head trying to rattle all the contradictions into place, "how could a man with no weapons in the car make four parallel slices from neck to groin?" I stabbed at the report in front of us with my index finger. "Slices so deep his intestines were found on the floor mat."

"Desperate people can do desperate things. You haven't been here long enough to understand."

"Maybe not, but I sure as hell know a cover up when I see it," I regretted that the second it blundered out, but I didn't appreciate his condescension. I was only trying to make my point The sounds on the tape were real, and no one would listen to me. The Sarge, whose face had transformed from warm bronze to weary gray since the start of the investigation, was tired of me pestering him.

"Look Anderson, the guy was stuck in traffic. He should have known the construction would hold him up, but no, he obviously wanted to make a grand exit. Once the traffic started up again," he flicked the report open to the witness statements and shoved it back toward me, "your cabby stayed put."

I knew what the report said. I'd memorized it along with my transcription of the tape. One angry driver came up to pound on the cab's window, but stopped when he saw blood smeared throughout the vehicle's interior. 911 was called, but for what? The gaping abdomen with intestines spilled across the front seat and onto the floor should have signaled the futility of an ambulance. Witnesses did hang around, people who were in the traffic jam beside and behind the cab. They reported seeing nothing unusual.

"Someone had to see something," I muttered.

"Who sees anything in this city? New Yorkers are too full of themselves and their own troubles to bother looking elsewhere. The only thing they notice are people like me. They pretend to be tolerant," his contempt filled my office, "but I can see the wariness in their faces as they try to figure out if I'm one of the dangerous '*Ay-rabs*' and wonder if I'm hiding a bomb under my jacket. And they aren't scared out of concern for the community, just fear for themselves and whether they'll make it home to show off their newest Prada accessory. Crimes happen all the time in broad daylight in this city and no one sees a thing."

"But you haven't listened to the tape," I persisted.

Was I seriously suggesting The Sarge listen to it? I hadn't let anyone listen to the tape. The whole recording is like a nightmare, but the sudden terror in the cabby's voice at the end and those sounds – sounds you don't hear in any nature film whether the antelope escapes or not – stick with you. I refused to let anyone else listen to it. Those who need the info read my transcript because I don't want anyone else to have to live with the haunting of those sounds.

But the Sarge was being stubborn. He slipped up and called it a murder when he was the one who insisted on declaring it a suicide in the official report. In my opinion, there had to be something more to it than what anyone was willing to admit. The tape is real and the victim's story is true, but the Sarge refuses to see it for what it is.

If only he heard the tape.

"If you'd just listen to the tape." His eyes narrowed at my insubordination. I continued in a meeker voice. "Surely the cabby's story will convince you."

"Your cabby was an aspiring writer. Every Arab has a little Ali Baba in him." I knew he meant Scheherazade, the teller of the tales of Ali Baba, but I kept quiet. I had other points to push. "We're worse than the Irish for telling superstitious tales. The tape will be held for evidence if anything comes up, but for now just drop it. Go back to your other work." He cast his eyes over my scattering of papers, recorders and tapes. "I don't want to hear any more of this. You bring it up again and you're out of here. You want to try to find a job in this economy?"

"No sir," I said.

"Good, then what did I say about this?" He stood and leaned with both hands on my desk to hover over me.

"Never bring it up again?"

"Never, ever. You do good work, Anderson. Don't let one silly tape get to you. He made it up. Get over it."

"Yes sir."

He turned to leave, but stopped halfway through the turn of the knob.

"If you go to anyone with this," he paused as if hesitating over the next card to play in a hand of poker, "I'll tell the department you had to leave for mental recuperation."

He finished the turn, yanked open the door, and strode out with an exhausted sigh.

~ ~ ~

The Sarge had tried to hush the investigation ever since I transcribed the tape. I wish I never had. I wish I could do as the Sarge said and never bring it up again, toss it away like a department memo; but whenever I'm not listening to music or TV or conversation that scream – *scream* doesn't convey the horror of the sound – plagues me. It's seeped into my skin and became a part of me like the ink of my tattoos.

The tape recorder, along with the remains of its owner, was found in City Cab 6473. The contents of that cab nauseated even Chief Tipps, the guy who proclaims he's seen it all. Two dread-filled lines -

"It's coming for me. Forgive me."

are preceded by the crinkling sound of safety glass being shattered.

Then the screaming begins.

Blending with the cabby's incessant shriek is a snarling - the snarl of a dog protecting a pork bone at the same time he's trying to eat it. Seconds later, there's a *swish* like a sword blade cutting through the air. The cabby's squeals of terror don't drown out the slopping fall of parts that were meant to be internal. And then silence.

But in your mind you still hear the screams

The Sarge needed to hear the tape.

I don't know why I felt so adamant about this. Normally I accept authority's demands and settle into my daily tasks. Plus, I liked the Sarge. Why did I want to battle him like a headstrong mule over this? I enjoyed my job and didn't want to lose it. The only problem I ever had at the Force was the mistake of asking one of the front desk girls out – little did I know then they all had crushes on the Sarge. Without hesitation, she rejected me citing the excuse that she didn't fish off the company dock and I foolishly believed her.

The next day, and every day for six weeks, whenever I walked past her and the other two, the trio of them watched me with faces tight from holding back silly grins. Once I was to the elevator, their repressed giggles would burst out. Eventually I gave up being embarrassed and instead greeted their stares with a charming smile - the Sarge's smile - and a "Hello, ladies" then walked on like I could care less. Two weeks later the girl asked *me* out. I told her I'd think about it.

What was it about this tape that would make me jeopardize my job, my relationship with the Sarge and getting to tease that receptionist?

It's just too real.

First off, it's not as if there was a foley sitting in the back seat conjuring these sounds; no one reported anyone entering or leaving the cab. Second, the cabby wanted to be a *writer*, not an actor. He couldn't fake such pure terror. I'm not sure even the world's best actor could. And third, I can't shake the notion that something on that tape needs to be understood.

If only the Sarge would listen.

I wasted several minutes staring at the report and walking the tape mindlessly across the desk from my phone to my lamp and back to the phone.

The phone.

I smiled at my own cleverness. I looked up the Sarge's home number. I knew his old one, but since his wife left him he'd gotten a new number to go with his new apartment. Before dialing, I checked my bank account - enough in savings for a few months of unemployment. My heart thudded so hard I could feel it in my fingertips, and with each digit I entered, I told myself I was crazy.

I paused on the last number. I could hang up now and be done. Do like he said and forget the tape. Weird shit happens all the time in this city. What would I accomplish by pressing that last digit? Who cares if some cab jockey goes down as a suicide?

I did.

Because I knew with more conviction than the certainty that my left nut hanging lower than my right that this was a murder - a murder that demanded an explanation. And I would force the Sarge to examine it.

I pressed the tenth number.

When the voice mail came on, I started the recording and switched to speakerphone to make sure I didn't get cut off.

~ ~ ~

The tape begins mundane enough. The voice is American, but with the slight accent of someone who spoke a different language at home as a child. Between fares our taxi driver was dictating a novel, and not a very good one. In mid-hyperbole he stops. The pause filled by a call like an eagle's screech mixed with the hoarse laughing of a hyena and, just faintly, you notice the clicking sound of dog's claws on pavement. Cabby 6473, forgetting his novel, begins again in a whisper:

"He's here. Dear Allah. I was drunk - Allah forgive me - that first night he came for me and I thought, I hoped, I imagined the thing, but it hasn't left me since. Always in my head I hear the 'tick-tick' of claws stalking me that night. I thought...I don't know what I thought. A dog, a loose mongrel following me for a handout, not this. Not what I saw. Not what's out there now."

His voice is shaking as if he's on the verge of crying. The car is idle. Stuck. Construction other cabs knew to avoid held him up. You hear the cabby inhale then exhale heavily to gain composure. He begins again in the murder-mystery tone from his earlier dictation, but underneath you can hear - especially if it's your job to listen – the slight tremble of fear.

"When I turned that night, my head spun with the liquor and I looked down to the level where I expected the dog to be. What would I have done if it were a dog? Shooed it away? Maybe kicked it just to get back at the world? But where a dog's back should have been were knees - dark knees, but not so black as to disappear into the night. The color of my father's knees. I prepared to be mugged and hopefully not beaten.

"If I felt tense at the sight of a man's knees following me in the dark, I was taut as a harp string when my eyes cast down and then, in an attempt to be bold, into his eyes. How I didn't scream I don't know. Perhaps too scared or too drunk to think it was anything more than vodka-inspired imagination. Allah knows I've sought inspiration for my stories in the bottom of a bottle more than once – Allah forgive me. I thought maybe this time it worked. I wasn't so lucky.

"My eyes flicked downward to the feet. Only a brief flash, but I knew what I saw and I knew why it sounded like a dog following. The feet were long thin things and he stood on the ends, the paws. The claws, like a dog's, weren't retractable.

"I see those claws now, just outside my window – why does he just circle the car like that? I've seen those claws every night in my sleep. The gleam makes it clear they are metal, sharpened to deadly points. The tapering edge on one side is surely a razor sharp blade."

The clicking continues outside the cab and, now that the cabby has put the concept in your mind, you can hear it isn't the dull tick of keratin, but a metallic clink, clink, clink.

"The face, what should have been a face, was a dog's elongated snout with the head of a Doberman. My stomach jolted as if hit with a lightning bolt."

The first time I listened I laughed at his cliché descriptions. The second time I shuddered. Now, I just listen with the hairs on my neck standing erect and wonder what the Sarge's reaction will be.

For the next few minutes our cabby seems to have talked himself out of his fear. He continues on in a swaggering tone punctuated now and then with a sarcastic snort

"The body was of a man, a well-muscled man wearing only a skirt of fabric over his loins. I wondered how he could stand it; it's January for Mohammad's sake. Then it clicked in my inebriated mind: Anubis, the Egyptian guide to the underworld. Suddenly sober, I stopped. 'I won't go with you,' I stated boldly.

"'It's time,' he said in his thick accent, the accent of my father, but with a throaty, ancient quality.

"I turned to stagger off and he let me, but I could feel his black eyes watching. Just as he watches me now, but that is all he does. Just watches. Some god.

"It couldn't be my time. I paid the gypsy woman for protection when I felt it coming. The lump in my belly, the inability to eat much. I knew these signs. I'd seen them in my father. He wouldn't go to the gypsies even though my mother urged him, and of course he wouldn't go to the American doctors who, in his words, 'Were more deadly than any cancer. Their exorbitant fees kill you by taking food from your mouth. What's the point of being cured if you can't eat?' And the gypsies, he wouldn't trust them. 'Only an Egyptian can cure an Egyptian,' he claimed.

"But I don't fall for that old nonsense. I can't afford the American doctors, but I can afford the gypsy woman's incantations and potions. I've paid her dutifully each week since feeling the lump, so Anubis cannot be coming to take me. Surely even gods can make mistakes.

"Besides, he only follows me. He never attacks because I bet he knows the gypsy woman protects me.

Still, his presence, his asking me to go with him and telling me that it's time gives me the feeling of mice scurrying up my back. I pretend not to listen and he continues to follow. He chases beside the cab every day barking at me that it will be worse if I don't go willingly with him. I won't. I saw him stalking me this morning. He'll never take me and to flaunt my assurance I'm going to the gypsy woman and paying her double.

"Now I sit here stuck in this traffic jam. I don't go this way normally, but the gypsy lives at the end of this street. I can get to her in time."

His voice loses its bravado on the last sentence and the quavering shimmy of fear resumes. I picture his chin trembling as he tries to keep talking.

"Why did I go this way? He's stalking the car now, circling it, the clicking of those claws grating in my ears as it has every time I've tried to sleep since I first saw him. Why does he look at me like that? He's crouching as if—"

At this point there's a thud. The cabby screams, not a fearful scream yet, but angry yelling at whatever it is to get off his cab. He curses at his demon. Our linguist, who I allowed to listen to only that portion of the tape, says it's Egyptian for calling the thing a son of a whore and telling it to go back to its world alone.

The safety glass crinkles in.

Blended with the cabby's scream is a savage snarling you hear deep down in your spine. The sounds are enough to feed my nightmares, but then come the last two lines. Six words spoken with unimaginably painful fear:

"It's coming for me. Forgive me."

More screams, the sound of flesh ripping, the wet slosh of intestines hitting the floor, and then silence. The hairs on my arms still rise at the sounds.

I shut the tape off. There's little more, just honking and people yelling to get out of the way, then the tape runs its course.

"Sarge," I say into the phone's speaker, "you have to believe this is more than suicide."

~ ~ ~

At two a.m. I'm wakened by a chiming noise. I can't place it until some portion of my mind tells me it's my phone. I pick up and, for whatever reason people do, try to sound like I wasn't sleeping.

"Hello?"

"Anderson? Did I wake you?"

The voice is the Sarge, but it's no tone I've ever heard from him. He's commanding, angry, cocky, but now —

He's been crying.

"No, Sarge, I'm awake." I was dying to ask if he got the voice mail, buy why else would he be calling me? "What's up?"

"You didn't have to do that. I believed you all along."

"Sir?"

"Look, Anderson," he sounded less tearful, but still low, hopeless even. "Legends of the old world aren't just legends. Some are true. Egyptians are bound to them almost genetically. The old gods didn't go away simply because so many decided to follow Mohammad. They wait their turn and do their job just as always."

He paused and then pushed out a rattling breath. I didn't interrupt with the thousand questions bombarding my mind. I let him gather his thoughts.

"Anubis, you know Anubis? Most Westerners know him even if he doesn't haunt them. He used to oversee funeral rites and then guided the dead to the underworld. Now we have no rights like the old ones for him to attend, but that damn jackal-headed god still insists on haunting the dying anyway. Even if we try to avoid it."

"We?"

"Those of us with terminal cancer. I never told you why Rita left, did I?"

"No sir."

"I got diagnosed with advanced lung cancer. Thought I gave up smoking in time, but apparently not. She said she couldn't go through watching me die and I didn't want her to. So we split. We're still married so she'll get my pension and all that. She knows what's coming for me, who's coming, and wants to stay out of his way. Our cabby's right, Anderson, sometimes even gods make mistakes and if she's around when he comes for me, he might take her too. Although, I hope he'll let me take my cat to the underworld. He does that, you know?"

"He who?"

"Anubis, you idiot. When it's my time he will come to guide me to the underworld. I'm scared a bit, but going with him willingly is like having someone hold your hand through a scary movie. The cabby fought it, tried to outwit a god and that's why Anubis took him the manner he did."

"So, in a way it was suicide?"

"I tried to tell you."

"I'm sorry, Sarge. I shouldn't have played the tape. I didn't mean to dredge up bad feelings."

"No, Anderson, thank you."

"For what?"

"I'm scared to die. Most people are, I'm sure. And I'm not ready. I'm only fifty-seven. I want to do more, see more, be with Rita more. So I thought of trying to avoid Anubis. I thought maybe it was just a legend. Why would anyone believe a creature with a jackal's head was wandering around taking Egyptians to their death? I certainly didn't. When this case came in though and I saw your transcription I thought perhaps the legends were true, but I still wanted to run to escape my fate. But the tape, you're right, the sounds are terrible. I don't want to face that. I'll let Anubis guide me when the time comes. It's the better way. I know that now. Thank you."

I didn't know what to say. I was on the verge of tears myself.

"You still there, Anderson?"

"Yes sir," my voice choked.

"You remember what I said?"

"About what?"

"Never bring this up again. We don't like our secrets to get out and don't want people investigating this or turning it into some cult. If you talk, if you spread this around, he will come for you too. Got it?"

"Yes sir."

~ ~ ~

The next day the Sarge didn't show up. He was declared dead of natural causes with death likely occurring between three and five in the morning. Forensics went to the apartment out of formality and I asked to tag along. Near the Sarge's bed I noticed marks as if four parallel knives had been pushed across the wood floor. I didn't point this out.

We never did find the Sarge's cat.

L'Uomo Cotto

"L'Uomo Cotto" popped out of my pen in a flash from a marathon of watching and reading Anthony Bourdain (Mr. B, if you ever read this, you'll notice your influence), my own obsession with overpopulation issues and, yet another, first line contest. Although you'll figure it out quickly enough, to not give anything away, I've kept the translation of the title until the end of the story. This story appeared in the 2011 anthology Soup of Souls.

Sam was a loyal employee. And cute too. Nico paused at his desk tapping the clicker of the ballpoint pen against his teeth then shrugged to himself accepting what had to be done. Damn shame, he'd miss the way her long blonde ponytail and tight ass swayed in motion together as she bustled between tables, but with the weekend rush, loyal or not, she had to be fired. He hated to do it, but he couldn't have her asking questions and, well, with times being what they were, it was the only way he could afford to stock the larders. He poured himself a drink, stared at the dropper bottle and waited for Sam's shift to end.

~ ~ ~

L'Uomo had been Nico's dream, hell, any chef's dream. After years of slogging away for other chefs, other managers and those damn owners who - despite never having stepped inside a professional kitchen - thought that they could start a restaurant because they whipped up a decent cassoulet, Nico finally took the plunge, shouldered the loans and opened L'Uomo.

Hopes and standards were high then. Customers sought sustainable and humane so Nico insisted on dolphin-friendly fish, local produce and free-range meat that met an ethical perfection even the clergy couldn't attain. It's not how he would eat, some of the stuff tasted like old dirt, but the richie riches in the affluent metro area dove in with pocketbooks gaping to gobble it up.

After hours the menu changed to his preferences and top local chef's honed in on L'Uomo to graze on oddities and rarities while imbibing Nico's range of Northwest microbrews, wines and - on those strange and somber winter evenings - absinthe. Upon his invitation, they flocked in like seagulls to scraps of bread. What higher achievement could he have asked for than other chefs choosing his place to hang out?

And one item - Nico's weakness - that kept them checking their email for his late night soirees was otolan: rare songbirds force fed to twice their healthy size, roasted in a cognac bath and eaten whole. None of the other chefs declined an invitation whenever this treat decorated the after hours plates at L'Uomo; they delighted in biting into the bodies as much as Nico did. There was something almost sexual, perhaps orgiastic, in the combined crunch of the tiny bones and harmonized sounds of pleasure as the juices filled their mouths.

"Ain't these things endangered?"

"Close to it, so enjoy," Nico replied.

"What wouldn't you eat, Nico?"

"Yeah, roasted any baby pandas lately?"

"If I cooked them, you know you'd like it," Nico said as he wiped his chin. "And if I said it was antibiotic and cruelty-free beef, my customers would pay $25 for three ounces of it."

"Hell yeah, I'd eat my grandmother if you cooked her, dude. She's still free-range, you know? Speakin' of weird, any of you think you'd ever eat human?"

"Just my girlfriend." A round of crude male laughter filled the room and all that remained of the ortolans' magic was the satisfied smacks as everyone licked their fingers.

Eight months. Eight months of success, hit reviews, loyal crowds and even a photo shoot for *Cuisine Magazine*. L'Uomo was hot. And then the economy flopped. Home sales plummeted, but optimists simply declared it a buyer's market. Problem was no one had money to be a buyer as the financial life of the city slumped, slouched and then dragged itself through the mud. Unemployment hit twelve percent and people stopped coming in droves to L'Uomo. They all claimed they loved the concept of eating organically, locally and ethically, but the empty wallets couldn't cough up enough greenbacks to pay for it.

Nico laid off most of his employees, keeping only his most loyal cooks. He even waited his own tables. The pricier cuts of meat vanished from the menu. The satisfying sound and smell of grass-fed lamb and pasture-wandering beef being fired on the stovetop grill no longer filled L'Uomo's kitchen. His menu now revolved around chicken. Ethically happy chicken, but still, just chicken. His cooks grew bored and surly with their culinary limitations and people were only willing to pay so much for something they could get at the Colonel's for a third the price.

By Nico's calculations, the restaurant had about seven weeks before his loans and cards would be maxed out trying to keep L'Uomo afloat. When the last two, the only two, customers left after lunch service he jabbed a cigarette into his mouth, lit it the second he was out of the building and strayed to the park joking to himself he better pick out a bench to sleep on for the eventual day his dream died.

He selected a bench and hunched over his lap dragging on the cigarette and watching the people. So many people. That was the problem, he mused to himself, there were just too many damn people. The number of humans swarming the planet disgusted him. They wouldn't need all this enviro-eco-sustainable crap if there weren't so many freakin' human mouths to feed. It's why people were so unhappy; even Nico with only one college biology class under his belt knew the more crowded an environment got, the more stressed and depressed its population ended up being. And here they were, miserable in an economic crisis, gang kids shooting each other, religious nut jobs killing anyone who didn't see things their way, diseases rotting people from the inside out and yet humans just kept breeding as if more people wouldn't cause more problems. Nico dropped the cigarette butt and smashed it out with his foot.

"I hope you're planning on throwing that away," a woman snipped. Nico looked up. She had that round on the way to fat look of someone who probably crawled inside an ice cream container every time she got upset. Three children followed her and twins babbled in a stroller. Nico observed the tell tale bulge of another bun in the oven and thought of that last ortolan feast.

"Yeah, lady, that cigarette butt is the problem."

He unfolded himself from the bench and walked away, determined to reinstate meat on L'Uomo's menu and turn his restaurant around. After all, meat was abundant and cheap if you knew where to look.

~ ~ ~

The help wanted sign Nico posted a week later brought in ten hopefuls the first day. Nico's easy manner led them to talk about a variety of things without him even asking. The happy, well-connected ones were passed over; they'd get jobs elsewhere more easily than the loners and introverts Nico hired on.

To fit more with the new direction of the restaurant Nico renamed it L'Uomo Cotto. And to remind people of L'Uomo's existence, Nico personally posted flyers at the houses and condos of his former loyal customers. The flyers promised lush meals with free-range meat, but priced to match the economy. Low prices, almost as low as the damn chicken. The first night, business was up by ten percent from the previous week. By the following week, it was nearly to the highest point he'd reached all those months ago.

People couldn't get enough. They smacked their lips on thin-sliced pancetta, delighted in the indulgence of crispy cracklin's and savored the porcine smell that reminded them of pork chop suppers and Christmas hams. Nico guaranteed his Jewish and Muslim clientele that the meat was not pig, just a common herd animal new to the culinary world.

Butchering the meat himself was hard work, but his training years ago with a seafood prep cook taught him how to cover every inch of a small storage room he'd cleared out and dubbed The Abattoir with plastic tarps to contain all the blood and funnel it into the room's floor drain. Once he separated the meat for the cooks, broke the bones for the stockpot and set aside organs for the more adventurous eaters, Nico rinsed The Abattoir in bleach and water and allowed it to dry. When the smell of chlorine greeted his cooks in the morning, they knew the larders would be filled again and looked forward to firing up the meat Nico called *maiale lungo*.

And, never bothered by not seeing the same wait staff more than a few times, the customers kept coming. Besides, everyone knew turnover was always high in the restaurant business.

Nico recalled the day Sam applied for a wait staff position. She was cute, smart, sexy in a meek sort of way and Nico couldn't believe she didn't have a boyfriend, girlfriend or any friends at all it seemed.

"I moved here for school and lost myself in books," she said in the interview. "I guess I didn't bother to set aside time to make friends or do stuff with other people."

"No family, sisters or brothers to keep you company?"

She shook her head no.

"Not even a cousin?"

"My parents died in a train crash on a trip through Europe when I was little. My grandma raised me, but she died last summer. That's why I thought I'd start over somewhere else."

She was perfect. Showed up on time, never talked back, respectful towards the cooks, but when he fired Katy, Sam started asking questions.

"Could you give me her number? I thought we got to be friends sort of and I'd like to keep in touch."

"I can't really give out personal information. If you want me to pass your number to her, I could do that."

When Katy didn't call, Sam started again.

"Why was she fired? She never did anything wrong."

Nico had a few standard responses this question. The cooks used to ask now and then when a waiter stopped showing up. They never pressed too hard though and eventually stopped asking altogether. They knew who commanded the kitchen and, as head chef, Nico's word was law in his own restaurant.

"She stole from the customers. Several times. One of the other wait staff noticed."

"I can't believe it."

"People have secrets in this business, Sam."

"But the other wait staff. No one seems to stay more than a couple months and whenever I ask your cooks they just say 'so and so was fired last night.' You do a lot of firing."

"It's how this restaurant stays afloat."

"But couldn't you give Katy a reprimand? A warning?"

"You're very defensive of someone who won't even call you."

"I just— She doesn't seem the type."

"Look, Sam, we need to start dinner service. Do you want to talk more about this after work?"

Sam's smile burst out from her fresh face. She never had anything to do after work.

"That'd be great."

Nico sat in his office clicking the pen, clicking the pen and staring at the dropper on his desk. Sam had to be fired. She was too smart. She'd figure it out eventually and then—

It'd be hard to prove anything he always supposed, circumstantial evidence sure, but rumor might get around and in a small city like Portland he'd be sunk on that alone. Nico refused to let his dream die. He'd brought L'Uomo back too strongly for it to collapse because of some college cutie. She had to be fired.

Sam knocked on the door.

"Come in." Nico took a sip of his whiskey to bolster himself. No matter how many times he did this, it didn't get any easier.

Sam entered. As she opened the door, Nico could see the lights were out in the kitchen. He indicated the chair opposite his desk. He took another sip of his drink.

"Want one?"

"Sure."

"Ever try absinthe?" Her eyes widened as if he'd just offered her heroin. She shook her head no and the ponytail swished back and forth along her neck. "Well, this will be my treat, It's distilled here in Oregon, you know?"

He set up the glass with a slotted spoon balanced across the rim, placed a sugar cube on the spoon's bowl and added a few drops from the dropper onto the cube.

"I've seen this in a Johnny Depp movie. It looked so cool and exotic."

"It'll change you, that's for sure."

He poured a small amount of water over the cube and the absinthe turned an opalescent green. Sam couldn't take her eyes off of it. With a flick of the spoon, the sugar plunked into the glass.

"There you go, enjoy."

Sam took a tentative sip and smiled. Nico never expected it, but she raised glass and tossed the entire contents back.

"Another?" he asked.

Before Sam could answer, she slumped forward, her head landing on Nico's desk with a thud. Nico pressed the intercom on his office phone. Silence. Everyone was gone and invitations to Portland's other chefs were never issued for the nights someone had to be fired.

Nico dragged Sam to the room at the rear of the kitchen and pulled out his key, the only key, to the Abattoir. He'd set up the plastic that morning. Meat stocks were low and someone was going to have to refill the larders. It was a shame it had to be Sam. Nico unlocked the door and dragged Sam in, her long blonde ponytail mopping limply behind across the floor. The knives glistened on the metal table ready to do their work. Tomorrow, when the grills fired up, Sam would be on them and the droves of paying customers would be satiated once again at L'Uomo Cotto.

~ ~ ~

L'uomo cotto = the cooked man

Maiale lungo = long pig

Self-taught Italian is so handy!

Special Thanks to...

My husband David who read these stories more than once as they were being written even though he's not a fan of fiction in any form.

And to the now-defunct Writer's Journal for delivering so many inspiring first lines.

And, apparently thanks are due to Anthony Bourdain who provided fodder for two of these tales.

About the Author

Tammie Painter worked for years in science before discovering her true passion in writing. Since taking the plunge to quit the day job and write full time, Tammie has had numerous articles published in local, national and international magazines and on various locales on the Internet. She has also won several awards for her essays and fiction.

Tammie is also the author of *Easy Preserving*, a humorous and informative guide to saving your garden's bounty and *Soup for You*, a collection of fabulous soup recipes (both available in print and electronic forms). Currently, she is hard at work on book on cheese making and a novel.

When Tammie breaks free from the chains binding her to her desk, she enjoys gardening, cooking, cycling, playing guitar, planning her next vacation and reading. Not all at the same time, of course.

To learn more about Tammie or to contact her, please visit her website

TammiePainter.com

Or follow her on Twitter @tammie_painter

Copyright

© 2012 Copyright by Tammie Painter and Black Rabbit Publishing. All Rights Reserved.

All rights reserved. No part of this book may be reproduced or transmitted in any form without written permission from the author, except in the manner of brief quotations embodied in critical articles and reviews. Please respect the author and the law and the rights of the author and do not participate in or encourage piracy of copyrighted materials.

Only the Publisher and authorized resellers have the right to resell this package subject to the terms and conditions given.

To contact the author or to learn about her upcoming books, visit:

TammiePainter.com

These stories are a work of fiction. Names, characters, places and incidents either are the product of the author's imagination or are used fictitiously and any resemblance to any persons, living or dead, business establishments, events or locales is entirely coincidental.

ISBN-13: 978-1479176175
ISBN-10: 1479176176

OFFICIALLY NOTED
Water damage

DISCARD

Milwaukie Ledding Library
10660 SE 21st Avenue
Milwaukie OR 97222

14303340R00114

Made in the USA
Charleston, SC
02 September 2012

52899960